Donald MacKenzie and Tl ⟶ _. ᵤₑᵣ Room

〉〉〉 This title is part of The Murder Room, our series dedicated to making available out-of-print or hard-to-find titles by classic crime writers.

Crime fiction has always held up a mirror to society. The Victorians were fascinated by sensational murder and the emerging science of detection; now we are obsessed with the forensic detail of violent death. And no other genre has so captivated and enthralled readers.

Vast troves of classic crime writing have for a long time been unavailable to all but the most dedicated frequenters of second-hand bookshops. The advent of digital publishing means that we are now able to bring you the backlists of a huge range of titles by classic and contemporary crime writers, some of which have been out of print for decades.

From the genteel amateur private eyes of the Golden Age and the femmes fatales of pulp fiction, to the morally ambiguous hard-boiled detectives of mid twentieth-century America and their descendants who walk our twenty-first century streets, The Murder Room has it all. **〉〉〉**

The Murder Room
Where Criminal Minds Meet

themurderroom.com

Donald MacKenzie 1908–1994

Donald MacKenzie was born in Ontario, Canada, and educated in England, Canada and Switzerland. For twenty-five years MacKenzie lived by crime in many countries. 'I went to jail,' he wrote, 'if not with depressing regularity, too often for my liking.' His last sentences were five years in the United States and three years in England, running consecutively. He began writing and selling stories when in American jail. 'I try to do exactly as I like as often as possible and I don't think I'm either psychopathic, a wayward boy, a problem of our time, a charming rogue. Or ever was.'

He had a wife, Estrela, and a daughter, and they divided their time between England, Portugal, Spain and Austria.

Henry Chalice

Salute from a Dead Man
Death Is a Friend
Sleep Is for the Rich

John Raven

Zalenski's Percentage
Raven in Flight
Raven and the Kamikaze
Raven and the Ratcatcher
Raven After Dark
Raven Settles a Score
Raven and the Paperhangers

Raven's Revenge
Raven's Longest Night
Raven's Shadow
Nobody Here By That Name
A Savage State of Grace
By Any Illegal Means
The Eyes of the Goat
The Sixth Deadly Sin
Loose Cannon

Standalone novels

Nowhere to Go
The Juryman
The Scent of Danger
Dangerous Silence
Knife Edge
The Genial Stranger
Double Exposure
The Lonely Side of the River
Cool Sleeps Balaban
Dead Straight
Three Minus Two
Night Boat from Puerto Vedra
The Kyle Contract
Postscript to a Dead Letter
The Spreewald Collection
Deep, Dark and Dead
Last of the Boatriders

Dangerous Silence

Donald MacKenzie

An Orion book

Copyright © The Estate of Donald MacKenzie 1960

The right of Donald MacKenzie to be identified as the author of this
work has been asserted in accordance with the Copyright, Designs and
Patents Act 1988.

This edition published by
The Orion Publishing Group Ltd
Orion House
5 Upper St Martin's Lane
London WC2H 9EA

An Hachette UK company
A CIP catalogue record for this book is available from the British Library

ISBN 978 1 4719 0565 0

www.orionbooks.co.uk

For my daughter Caroline

I

The four-fifty down from Waterloo stopped at Two Bridges as it always did, Monday through Friday, the locomotive square with the station sign, the three first-class carriages facing the exit. Fraser slammed the heavy door behind him and sprinted for the barrier. He brushed by the red indignant face under its uniform cap, moving a hand in token gesture.

The small booking-hall was sad with broken vending machines, improbable posters and a dank cement floor. An incessant rain drummed on the roofs of the cars parked outside in the station yard. A solitary cab-driver sat behind swishing windshield wipers like some disconsolate fish in a tank.

The other passengers were crowding into the exit behind Fraser. He ducked into the rain, squelching the length of the yard. He stood there under a dripping overhang. Screened by a half-open door he had a clear view of the booking-hall exit.

Now I'll know, he told himself. In a couple of minutes I'll be sure. There had been no chance of certainty at Waterloo. A dozen yards had separated him from the man he had followed through the barrier there. No time for more than a glimpse of jawline—an impression of stooped, ponderous height. Yet enough to keep Fraser hidden in the lavatory till the train left the station. Later he found his usual seat and rode the twenty-eight miles to Two Bridges with averted head. Neck stiff with apprehension. Suddenly conscious of a world avoided yet never forgotten.

Men were stepping into the driving rain as he peered through the crack in the door. Fraser counted them as if in this way he might exclude the one he feared. He knew these people by sight if not by name. Middle-aged men in city clothes—each a little ridiculous in his purposeful sprint to the line of waiting vehicles.

Behind the brick wall at Fraser's back, the train was rattling over the switch at the reservoir. Water cascaded from the gutter overhead spreading a damp patch across his shoulders. Two cars were left in the yard. His own Buick and a waiting cab.

He edged forward, suède shoes welt-high in a puddle. Kline might still be on the train now screaming through the Green Hill Cut. There were five stops between Two Bridges and Portsmouth. But as if on cue, the last passenger appeared in the booking-hall doorway. He stood like some monstrous predatory bird. Wide shoulders stooped, he leaned from his great height, shielding his bare head from the rain. A short hooked nose jutted over a full mouth. He wore grey hair close to the scalp in a series of tight springs. As Fraser watched, Kline lifted an arm to hold it in a near-Roman salute. He held it there till the cab driver manœuvred his vehicle to the door. Kline spoke to the driver then leaned back, shutting his eyes as though he slept.

Fraser peered through the slit till the cab topped the rise from the yard. It turned east towards the village. The station was quiet once more. Fraser ran to the Buick. Inside he followed the routine of years. Tossing the brief-case to the back seat, kicking his right foot free of its shoe —turning the ignition key till an eye glowed red on the dashboard.

He used reason to fight the shake in his hand. Maybe

2

Kline's presence in Two Bridges was no more than coincidence—it was a chance. Instinct was stronger than reason and he sat in the dark car wet and unsure.

After six years it had caught up with him—not as he had always feared, by accident.

There'd been four hundred men with him in jail. During those first few weeks the drab grey uniform had a protective anonymity blurring the faces of those who wore it. That was the beginning. By the time he had finished his sentence, he'd known his comrades too well. Worked, walked and ate with them for two years. He had come to know each man's story intimately. Suffered the inevitable recital of misfortune or treachery, never of incompetence. It had been a long two years with his personal decision taken with less thought for ethics than expediency. Given just one lucky break, he'd reasoned, a man with intelligence might earn a great deal of money legitimately.

For an ex-con to achieve respectability the Fate Sisters *had* to be kind. Every man in the jail was a threat for the future. The denunciation might come from the waiter who served you soup—with the match offered hoarsely from the shadows—the face in a bar suddenly no longer that of a stranger. But always, he'd told himself, it would come fortuitously.

Now this. Six years was a long time. Not till you remembered the old values did you discover you'd acquired new ones. Not overnight—with *mea culpas* brayed down your nose—but imperceptibly. And if the old fears had persisted it was because there was more to lose now.

He started the motor and turned the convertible up the slope. Back wheels spun as he took the bend fast, snatching the car into second gear. A mile towards the village, he caught sight of tail-lights through the driving rain. He knew every inch of the highway and slowed on the straights, making time on the bends. There was little enough of Two Bridges. A score of cottages built around a green. A small Norman church, its vicarage hidden by a clump of elms. Two pubs and the village store. A lone street lamp threw a pale early beam to the edge of the soaked green.

He ran the car into the shelter of the churchyard wall. Beyond the stone memorials dotted with dead flowers, somebody was at organ practice. The cab had stopped in front of the *Dog and Fox*, a half-timbered inn whose lack of neon lighting was an obvious concession to the neighbourhood. Kline was standing in the doorway, coat draped about his shoulders. As he sought change, the empty sleeves flapped. He waited till the cab turned towards the station then walked into the lighted bar.

Fraser moved the car to the vicarage gates. Here it was completely hidden from the pub. He tucked up his trousers, turned up his jacket collar and squelched down the driveway. A stable yard at the side of the inn was used as a parking lot. Once through the arch, he picked his way across slippery cobbles. A light shone through cracks in the bar curtains. Huddled in the foul lavatory, he watched the arch and street. Then, flat against the wall, he worked his way to the first window.

The room was empty except for Kline and the woman behind the bar. The lawyer had his back to her. He was holding his coat to the fire. After a moment, Kline crossed the room. Even at twenty yards and without benefit of sound the gallantry was theatrical. His drink served, Kline carried it to a seat by the fire and sat staring, chin in hand.

Suddenly he looked at his watch and swung his head

towards the woman. She nodded, pointing at a door that led to the lobby. Bending, Kline ducked under a sign that read TELEPHONE. Hobnails were scuffling the cobbles from the direction of the street. Fraser moved from the window quickly and walked towards the sound. An oil-skinned farm labourer grunted greeting.

Back in the car, Fraser considered his next move. Kline belonged to the very start of Fraser's burglary rampage. An assault on property that had involved the police forces and insurance companies of three countries. The lawyer had been part both of its beginning and its end. His appearance in Two Bridges would be with purpose backed with intelligence. And a ruthlessness for those who no longer lived as he lived.

Fraser drove fast up the hill, past the station. On till he skidded the convertible into his own driveway. There he parked under the dripping trees. Out of sight of the house where he and Barby had lived since their marriage.

Those first weeks out of jail, six years ago, fortune seemed to have worked in his favour. He had been in Canada House, the day he met Barby. The weekly visit to collect mail that never came. Secretly he knew there never *would* be a letter from home. Three thousand miles away, the doors in the house on the river had been shut irrevocably. For Barby, the visit had been a routine chore. It was the year her parents made a trip through the Canadian Rockies. He had first seen her, standing at the Inquiry Desk, clutching a batch of travel folders. There had been some question of a pen. A second's hesitation and she took the one Fraser offered.

After a week of constant meetings he gave her his story without embellishment. Recalling a rebellious childhood without regret or excuse. It all seemed so far away.

Escape to a war that brought uncertain glory. A so-called hero turned burglar. A career as sudden in its ending. He had made the recital deliberately, knowing that it could ruin his chance of happiness with her. He told it because he must.

They were eating at one of the Chelsea coffee-bars. She kept her voice low, leaning across the table. " I'm glad you've told me. I'd have hated it if you hadn't! But you've got to promise me one thing—that you'll never repeat this to anyone else. Certainly not to my parents. Or to the people I know. Not even to the people *you* know." She cupped one of his hands in hers. " Listen to me, Kit! *Nothing* can change the feeling I have for you. That's what I believe, anyway. It's happened bewilderingly fast but I know that one of us has to keep a level head. I've got to think about the future. So have you. If you told this story to my father—if he thought it happened to somebody else—he'd be kind and charitable." She pulled his hand to her breast, forcing him to listen. " If you said it was your story, he'd throw you out of the house. It isn't that he's cruel, Kit. But I'm his daughter."

He used sarcasm to cover the hurt. " Possibly. But you have some sort of stake, I imagine. There's the chance he'd cut you off with a penny. That's the classic phrase, isn't it ? "

Her eyes had been shut in exasperation. Now she opened them wide. " Now *you* listen. I've heard a lot about 'expediency' since I've known you. As far as I can see, you use it as a sort of justification for your contempt for other people's beliefs. But anyway—its *expedient* that you put everything you've told me out of your head for ever." She blocked his protest. " Be sensible, Kit. You talk about marriage but you haven't even got a job let alone a home!"

He swished the black sweet dregs in his cup—drained them. "The same old wail! Security!"

She shrugged impatiently. "What's *wrong* with security! For you as well as for me! We can both have it if you give my father the chance to think I'll be happy with you."

His chair rasped back. He was indifferent to the interest of the couple at the next table. "That sounds real jolly! 'I'd like you to meet my son-in-law. We don't really know much about the boy—he's been a rolling stone but only in the best sense of the word, of course.'" Seeing the shock in her face, he lowered his voice. "What sort of start would a marriage get on those terms?"

Her eyes were hidden behind her hand mirror. "And if they were the *only* terms, Kit?"

He made no answer. They walked in silence through quiet Belgravia streets to the house in Westminster. She gave him her hand when they reached the end of the short street. "Good-bye, Kit!" Her meaning was plain.

For a long time, after she had gone, he stood in the shadow. Watching the room he knew was hers. A light came then went quickly. He started back to his room on Walpole Street. At Sloane Square he stopped and called her from a booth. They were married three months later.

This house through the trees, still gay with red roof and white paint in spite of the rain, had been her father's wedding present. Six long years back. He'd come a long way since then with Patterson, Gilchrist and Todd. Not that it had been too tough. With his father-in-law's approval, most of Fraser's accounts were found outside the Suffolk Street office. What the Old Bailey judge had called " a spurious charm coupled with complete lack of principle " seemed to have its place in brokerage circles. Last year alone, Fraser had brought in more than one hundred and fifty thousand pounds' worth of business. All of it burglary insurance. Somehow the irony of the situation became less amusing because it could never be shared. Yet he had lived honestly. A cop now was at worst a man with a parking ticket—or Simmonds the village constable, flushed with embarrassment, selling tickets for the police dance.

He hit the starting button again. No. The house ahead and the woman in it had given him back the things he had lost. An easy conscience and the right to sleep at night, undisturbed. He had to fight as he may for these things, come a dozen like Kline.

He turned the car on to the gravel patch between front door and rain-flattened grass. He bleated the horn a couple of times. Lights were burning pink-warm in the living-room. He waited as he always did till Barby waved from the window. Then he ran the car into the garage. He used the back door, kicking sodden shoes to the kitchen floor. As he donned slippers he became aware of the smells, the sounds, that made this home.

Barby was waiting in the living-room. Even in stockinged feet, her gangling height almost matched his own. He held her at arms' length for a moment. " I just remembered," he said solemnly. " You're a dish to come home to ! "

She broke his hold. Dabbed his neck with her lips. She wiped the stain with a handkerchief. " Branded," she said with satisfaction. Her smile went beyond the full mouth to the sun-creased skin at the corners of her eyes. Straight brows matched hair the colour of a late October maple-leaf. She wrinkled a nose which was too short. " My God! You smell exactly like a wet dog!" She touched his jacket. " Kit, you're soaked!"

He flung his suit coat at a chair; " I had trouble with the car door. Stood in the rain looking for the right key."

She was hanging his coat in the hall closet. " Then I'm not the only one who does it!" she called.

He was on the couch, his feet up. The curtains were not yet drawn. The rain had stopped outside. A blackbird swung under the bird-perch, ramming its beak greedily at the coconut. In the fading light the still clump of firs had density. The only sound came from a spattering log in the fireplace. This house had been built for them, he remembered. And Barby had chosen every stick in it. Week-ends, they'd driven to offbeat country sales—searching jumbled lots with the excitement of children faced with a Lucky Dip. It was difficult to imagine anyone else living in the house they had watched grow. Leaving it was a disaster that he shut from his mind.

He closed his eyes, his voice carefully casual. " What happened today ? Who got born or buried ?"

She fixed his drink as he liked it. A third Scotch in a cut-glass tumbler, soda from their cartridge syphon. Her own drink she sipped as if it were medicine. A trick she affected with her first drink of the day.

" What happened ?" she considered. " Well for one thing Mrs. Ellis fused the lights again with the vacuum. I had the Gilmour children for Pony Club instruction. *Not* wildly amusing. A half-hour in the pouring rain and a session afterwards with Kate Gilmour. Jim's drinking." She sighed. " Mummy phoned. She wants me to meet her for a show this week. Then there was a call for you a

9

few minutes ago." She fed the fire logs. Two pine, one apple.

He kept his eyes tight shut. " A call for me! Who was it ? " He felt the sudden warmth as the wood caught fire.

" Some man," she answered indifferently. " Nobody I ever heard of. A business call, he said." She stood behind him, kneading his neck muscles.

" He must have had a name," he said cautiously. He opened his eyes as he heard her cross the room.

She read from the pad in front of her. " Kline. K-l-i-n-e. He was most particular that I got the spelling right."

He swung his feet to the floor. " I'll put on some dry things." At the foot of the stairs he stopped, trying for an indifference to match hers. " This guy leave any message ?"

Her answer came from the kitchen, almost drowned by running water. " He said he'd call back later. I told him you were usually home about six. Fine, he said. You'd know who he was. Conversation finished." Her voice stopped him half-way to the bedroom. " Kit!"

He gripped the stair rail till his fingers hurt. He cracked on the answer and had to repeat it. " What ?"

" I thought we'd eat early," she called. " There's boxing for you on Channel 2."

He changed his clothes quickly. The light wool shirt was a reminder of long winter evenings, the two of them content in the firelit room below. He had a foot in a dry sock when the phone bell split the quiet of the house like a buzz-saw. He lifted the receiver, stilling the summons. When he had kicked the door shut, he sat quietly in the deep chair. White paint glinted in the twilight. The room was sharp with Barby's scent. He put an ear to the instrument.

The voice was deep and pleasantly modulated. " Good-evening. May I talk to Mr. Fraser, please ?"

It might have been yesterday, in the office high over Park Lane. Across the desk in the panelled Adams room, Kline. A little thinner maybe but with the same strength to soothe, to twist and lie. " So there it is, Kit. I'll meet you outside the Old Bailey to-morrow at half-past nine. You have to surrender to your bail through the court. And remember—" The lawyer stood, fine boned hands on polished wood taking the weight of his body. " Leave the worrying to me! That's what you pay me for."

He'd seen Kline just once more after that. In the cells, after sentence. The good warm handshake was still there—the confident smile. " We'll beat 'em on appeal, Kit. It's a matter of waiting a few weeks. No more. We'll get one of the really big men—somebody like Moriarty. Somebody the Lord Chief won't dare to browbeat. Oh, and Kit." Kline sighed, mocking his own importunity. " I'm afraid it's going to cost you money."

There had *been* no money. And no appeal. Not even a letter from Kline. As time went by the lawyer faded into a sour memory. Five years afterwards, the headlines that dealt with Kline's personal appearance in the dock had changed nothing. Friends were too few for their treachery to be erased even by their own misfortune.

He put his mouth close to the instrument, keeping the antagonism out of his voice. " It's me, Kline."

" Kit!" There was just the right combination of pleasure and surprise. " How soon can I see you ?"

" What do you want to see me about ?"

" Look—" The tone was still friendly. Just a little

11

hurt. "It's been a long time for us both, Kit. You weren't too easy to find." Kline laughed.

Yes, a long time, he thought. He wet his lips. "All right. You've found me. Now what do you want?"

"A chat," said Kline. "Just a chat for old times' sake. I'm here in the village. At the *Dog and Fox*." Command crept into the lawyer's voice. "How soon can you get here?"

Somehow he must contrive to isolate this threat—keep his home free of Kline's menace. He answered. "Fifteen minutes. Look—I don't want you to call this number again. That's important. Never! Do you understand, Kline?" The line was dead.

The clock chimed a couple of times as he made his way down the stairs. Crockery was chinking in the kitchen. He waited in the hall. The truth here would be a nice touch for Barby. "The man who just phoned used to be my lawyer. A great guy who nursed me through a dozen police interrogations. Who set up the three best hauls I ever made. My pal Kline, the friendly backstabber. I'm going down to the pub now to have a drink with him for old times' sake."

All right—the truth without being comic. How was this. "There's a guy in the village asking for me. Christ knows I'm scared to go but I'm even more scared *not* to go!"

He laced on a pair of waterproof brogues. Perhaps he was hollering before he was touched. Let the explanations wait. First find out what Kline wanted.

The kitchen was the inevitable shambles that was Barby's background for a meal. Tottering pans, bottles that leaned at crazy angles from the open refrigerator. There was a good smell. She was wearing a ridiculous

checked apron and a swatch of hair over her nose. She
gave the kitchen clock a hard look as he came in.
" Supper's ready in fifteen minutes. Was that your
chum ?"

He poured ice-cold milk, sipped it to gain time. " Uhuh.
He's in the village and wants me to meet him there for a
half-hour. Now look, Barby!" He held up a hand. " I
swear I won't be longer."

" A half-hour!" She used a spoon to push the hair
from her eyes. She pointed at the stove. " What am I
supposed to do with *that*!"

He rinsed the glass carefully and set it in the drying
rack. " It's something I can't very well get out of, darling.
It's a big account—a new one and the man has no time."

When she frowned she had a nervous trick of lifting her
chin. " Why can't you bring him back here ? If he
doesn't like *scampi*, he can go hungry."

There was a battery of pot handles between them. He
righted each one and kissed her cheek; " I want to *get*
this account, not lose it," he kidded. He held a finger to
her nose. " A half-hour."

Outside, a west wind was up, drying the trees. The
Buick's tyres swished over macadamed roads. In the
village he parked out of sight at the rear of the stable
yard. Hidden in the car, he rifled through his wallet,
leaving two five-pound notes and a one. The rest of his
money he locked in the glove compartment. If Kline's
purpose was a swift touch, better that he saw no car—no
more than a modest bankroll.

Inside the pub the lounge was stereotype for that part
of the country. Horse-brass and John Gilpin's Ride.
Behind the bar pewter tankards on numbered hooks.
Kline was still in front of the old turnspit fireplace, his

back to the door. The woman took Fraser's order with the familiarity of the genteel tavern keeper. " A large one, Mr. Fraser ? Let's see—it's the Haig & Haig, isn't it ?" She pushed the syphon at him. " And how's that pretty wife of yours ?"

Kline had turned at the sound of voices. Fraser crossed the room. Apart from the woman, they were alone in the bar. Kline posed his drink. Hand outstretched, he leaned forward, his face ruddy in the firelight. " Kit! This is splendid!"

Fraser lifted his drink, avoiding the hand. " Let's sit down," he said. The corner settle seats were as far as possible from the bar. He kept his voice low, his face turned towards the other man. " I'm not going to ask any of the things you probably expect, Kline. How you managed to find me—stuff like that. Just one question—what do you want ?"

Kline's fingers, his nails, were immaculate. But he gave them careful consideration. " I suppose one might call it help," he said mildly. " I prefer the term co-operation."

" The sort of co-operation you gave me ?" Fraser's lighter was useless. Kline touched a match to the cigarette. Fraser held his wallet open but hidden from the bar. " There's a tenner, here, Kline. Take it and go back where you came from!" He folded the two bills and slid them under the ashtray. " Forget you ever knew me," he added.

Kline left the money there. " That could have been a friendly gesture," he said quietly. " But it wasn't." He touched the back of his head then leaned his height nearer Fraser. " We're going to have to start all over again, Kit, you and I. With no hard feelings about what happened years ago. You never heard my side of the

14

story. Never will!" His voice was sad. " I've been to jail myself since then, Kit."

" I read," Fraser said shortly. A noisy group had come in. The room was suddenly resonant with Staff College accents. " A tenner, Kline," he repeated. He sought for words that would register. " Get this right—next time you bother me, I'll call the law."

The older man finished his drink unhurriedly. He ordered another, bowing courteously when the woman brought it. " Tripe!" he said with contempt when she'd gone. " And what do you propose to tell the police—an old friend has looked me up—lock him away, please." His grey head wagged. " *Really*, Kit!"

" I've come a long way . . ." Fraser started. Something in the other man's face stopped him. " What is it you want from me, Kline?" he asked.

A trial dart thudded into the board three feet away. Still courteous, Kline waved permission at the players. He and Fraser moved to the other corner. " This isn't going to be pleasant, Kit." The man's gift for vocal sincerity was tremendous. " But you'll have to listen. You say you read my case in the newspapers." He spread both hands, head bowed. " Prison—disbarred—penniless. I'm fifty-six, Kit. It isn't easy to make a new start at that age."

"I'm in tears," Fraser said shortly. Once said, it was regretted. One thing he'd learned in jail—a man only goes straight when he has an alternative way of living. Doubt weakened his sarcasm. Kline's brain had never been suspect, only his use of it. Suppose he found the ex-lawyer a job—some business connection too far removed for it to matter if the recommendation went sour.

" If a job's really what you want," he said slowly, " it's just possible I could help."

15

" I said I'm too old to make a fresh start." The pupils
of Kline's eyes had white circles round them. Fraser
found himself trying to remember what eyes like that
were supposed to denote. The lawyer dusted ash from his
jacket fastidiously. " No," he said softly. " My talents
. . ." his hand deprecated the boast. ". . . my *gifts* are
still of some use. No. I have a backer, Kit. A young man
—very much like the one you used to be. Good family
background. Brains. And above all guts." He nodded
judiciously. " He'll go far. I'm going with him, Kit.
Which is where you come in!"

Fraser looked at his watch. Three-quarters of an hour
had gone by since he left the house. " I'm going home,
Kline. I'll wish you good luck. God knows whether I
really mean it."

The lawyer's hand plucked Fraser's sleeve, his voice a
whisper. " Insurance!" Fraser sank back in his seat, his
eyes never leaving the older man's face. " It's taken five
months to find you, Kit," continued the lawyer. " It's
been like solving some enormous crossword puzzle.
Piecing together newspaper cuttings—headwaiters' gossip.
Three weeks alone spent going through telephone direc-
tories." He tapped Fraser's arm. " You sell insurance.
Burglary insurance. For your father-in-law. Patterson,
Gilchrist and Todd, 120 Suffolk Street. You're married
and live in a very pleasant house among the trees, a few
miles up the road. And you own the blue Buick that was
parked in the station yard this evening."

Fraser touched handkerchief to a mouth suddenly dry.
He tried for words to stop what was coming.

Kline's lips were close to Fraser's ear, barely moving.
" Your firm insured a woman against burglary for eighty-
five thousand pounds. Last May. Mrs. Chester Garrett.

That's what my partner and I want, Kit. The terms of the Special Conditions clauses from that policy."

" The Special Conditions clauses," Fraser repeated stupidly. " You have to be out of your mind." The lawyer's eyes were implacable. Fraser tried to obliterate memory of the steel files at Suffolk Street—as though his expression would betray him. Every policy he had ever negotiated was kept there. Too well he knew what the other meant.

" You have access to all these papers," Kline urged gently. " Whether you handled the account yourself or not. You see, I know the game, Kit. For that amount of insurance, your father-in-law will have gone to one of the Lloyds syndicates. They'll have sent a surveyor to inspect the house. Locks, bolts and bars—the lot. And if their man wasn't satisfied, the underwriters will have added security measures of their own. All of it's there in the policy. Isn't it, my boy ?"

There was only confusion in Fraser's mind. Here and there certain words registered violent alarm. " You crazy bastard!" he said suddenly. Heads turned in the bar. He stayed as he was—half out of his chair. His hands were twitching and a hammer beat at his head. Kline laughed good-humouredly. It was public acceptance of a storm in a bar-room. He wrapped a heavy arm round Fraser's shoulder and led him to the door. The woman waved them good night from the bar.

In the shadows outside, they stood toe to toe, expectantly. Kline was first to break silence. " This is my last chance at really big money. I don't care how dirty I get, my boy. I'm ready to go to your wife—your father-in-law—if you force me. Tell them the fascinating story of your past from the first day we ever met." A carriage

17

lamp swung in the wind, a few yards away. Kline's eyes showed merciless in the brief light. He wagged his head. " Patterson's not the sort of man you'd have told your story to! Brooks's Club—Freeman of the City—a Justice of the Peace!" He moved a step nearer. " I don't suppose for a minute you've told that girl you're married to either. You'd have too much at stake with both of them." He pulled his sloping shoulders square. " I don't give a damn if you did." He grinned. " Once the Committee at Lloyds know an ex-con's been underwriting burglary insurance, they'll ruin the lot of you. Father-in-law included."

The group from the bar had come outside. They stood in the light of the lamp, loud and jovial. Fraser started for the car, moving mechanically. Kline followed. The two men sat in the stuffy darkness, already bound in conspiracy. Fraser lit a cigarette, blowing the smoke in nervous bursts. Beside him, the lawyer's breath came and went asthmatically.

" You can't screw up people's lives and get away with it," Fraser said unsteadily.

Kline grunted. " Spare me the moral indignation. It's out of place."

Fraser slumped lower in the seat, sliding his hand deep in the pocket of the door. When his fingers touched the smooth steel wrench, he drew them away. Neither moral indignation nor violence would help him. Only cunning. He spoke quietly, his tone an acceptance of defeat. " I can raise four thousand pounds. No more. Half of it's yours on one condition."

The lawyer was fiddling with an electric button, sending the window up then down. " I'm the one who makes the conditions, Kit. You'll have to remember that. I've told you what I want. Unless I get it, you leave me no alternative." He grunted again, twisting his body to face Fraser. " I under-estimate nothing about you, Kit. Your intelligence or your nerve. But short of killing me, there's nothing you *can* do. And you've far too much sense for that." His voice wheedled. " Look, Kit. We can make a fortune with complete safety. I know all about this woman's jewellery. It's mostly diamonds—gem quality diamonds. If anything, it's under-insured. It'll sell up for a guaranteed sixty thousand pounds. It means that I can sit out what's left of my life, somewhere in the sun. And you'd never hear of me again."

He had to get away from this coaxing assurance. Get away before he betrayed himself. The cunning he needed was blunt with disuse. He'd lived too fat and too easily. " I've got to have time," he said. " I've got a wife. . . . I've got to have time. . . ."

The lawyer checked his watch. " You've always found me reasonable enough, haven't you ? Drive me to the station. I can catch the six-fifty-two back to town. I'll meet you at two to-morrow. *Jacques Bar*—it's quiet there." He heaved his bulk so he could look at the dark-ened sky. " Quiet," he repeated.

The motor raced as Fraser rammed the nose of the Buick at the arched exit. As he slowed for the turn to the station, the speedometer needle was nudging seventy. People with problems sometimes wrapped themselves round a pole, he thought. Intentionally. There had to be other solutions. He braked in front of the booking-hall.

Kline climbed out ponderously to lean back through the window. " Till two to-morrow then. There's **one** thing I seem to have forgotten. You're on a full share **in** this venture, of course. Good night!"

19

When the lights of the train were gone Fraser slammed a fist at the dashboard. Glad of the pain of bleeding knuckles, he leaned his head against the steering-wheel. The sudden horn blare brought a curious porter to the booking-hall door. Fraser wrapped skinned flesh in a handkerchief and drove off, one eye on the mirror. The jungle was never too far away. Protective instincts were working already. Six years seemed to mean nothing to them. To-morrow he'd be back in a world of fear and suspicion. The unexpected phone call—the casual summons—part of a gauntlet that he must run alone. That was worst of all. He had put himself in a position where none could help him.

The curtains were drawn in front of the house. He backed the car into the garage and washed his hand there. Finding the first-aid kit, he taped a patch on his broken knuckles. No matter how he handled Kline, Barby had to be kept in ignorance. Her reaction would be inevitable. Call the police, she'd say. She'd be so sure she was right, she'd be capable of calling them herself. He had the certainty that this was one time when the police would be useless. Up to now Kline hadn't made a move that might be used in evidence against him. Not that manœuvring the lawyer into jail would settle anything. A letter from prison would reach Lloyds as certainly as from anywhere else. The solution lay somewhere between the threat and its execution.

He walked into the kitchen ready with his first lie. Barby was in the living-room. The lights were out—the place snug in the fireglow. She sprawled deep in the arm-chair, watching the flames snake up the wide chimney. Reading the signs, he walked back to open and shut the door with exaggerated pantomime. " That means I'm

home," he said wearily. " Ready to be noticed." He
snapped on the wall-lights.

She stretched her arms above her head. " Come here!"
she ordered. When he leaned down, she locked both
hands behind his neck. " You are a fool," she smiled. She
tugged, bringing his face nearer. " The *scampi*'s ruined—
fish-flavoured rubber by now."

The low table was cheerful with blue and yellow linen.
As she dropped a slice of bread into the toaster it fell to the
floor. *Gauche* as a schoolgirl at times, he thought with
sudden irritation.

" The motor cut out at the bottom of the hill," he said
defensively. " God knows I'm no mechanic."

She was pointedly indifferent. Holding a glass to the
light—wiping it free of some imaginary speck. " There's
a bottle of wine on ice in the kitchen." She put the glass
down with quick concern. " What did you do to your
hand ?"

" Try finding a busted lead in pitch darkness," he said
curtly. He followed her to the kitchen. Clumsily, he drove
the corkscrew in off-centre. Cuttings floated in the pale-
gold liquid. Because he knew she was watching, he kept
his head down. The worm in his forehead had become a
pulse. He had to sleep. Relax in the darkness as soon as
he could. He wrapped a napkin round the bottle and
carried it into the living-room.

All this sweetness and light, he thought hopelessly.
This decency and fairness over a ruined meal. With
Kline barely out of the village. He had the urge to shock
her free of belief in a world where all was black and white.
Where rogues purged their punishment while their betters
applauded righteously. Only it wouldn't do anything.
Those fixed ideas would persist. She couldn't help it.

Sooner than compromise, she'd accept destruction of everything they'd created together.

They ate behind drawn curtains, each apprehensive of the other. The table cleared, she stood hesitant, then switched on the television set. On the screen, gloved fighters pawed at one another ineffectually. With the commentator's first dramatic words, Fraser spun the control. The wine bottle was empty. He poured himself brandy.

Barby sat on the rug at his feet, her long legs drawn up, hands clasping her knees. " The temperamental Master Fraser," she said quietly. " What's the matter, Kit ?"

He worried the words like a dog a rat. " *What's the matter* ? What *should* be the matter ? We give this goddam thing a rest for just one evening in our lives and you're looking for tragedy !" The brandy caught at his throat but he emptied the glass determinedly.

Barby cried rarely. If she did, it was done with reason and in secrecy. But now she moved away quickly to poke flame into the fire. He watched her sombrely. Kline, he thought. Just as surely as though the lawyer had cut her across the face, Kline was responsible for her misery.

She took a hold on his ankle, spanning it with her fingers. She leaned her head against his knee. " *I loathe* that man you went to see," she said savagely. " I *hate* him! Running his beastly business into our home. I only wish. . . ."

He was suddenly incapable of controlling the hysteria in his voice. " Stop it, Barby," he shouted. " For Christ's sake, stop it !" Shaking, he poured himself another drink When he turned round she had moved to the other armchair.

" What *is* the matter with you, Kit ?" she demanded.

22

He looked at her vaguely. Desperately he wanted some-one else to share the blame. If it hadn't been for her goddam peace of mind he wouldn't have *been* in a position of trust with a half-told secret. And supposing he'd gone to Patterson with the truth. There was still the Committee at Lloyds. And an ex-con writing burglary insurance. But there wouldn't have been any job then. He'd have had no value for Kline.

" I'll tell you what it is," he said heavily. " I'm tired. Five days a week—forty-eight weeks a year—the same old thing." He raised his glass, grinning ironically. " Weasel-ing introductions to those old bags your father keeps listed. Waltzing like a bloody performing dog." He bounced his hand in the air. " Up, Fraser! Down, Fraser!"

She sat up straight, chin lifted, her brows a straight bar above her eyes. " My father never forced you to do any-thing, Kit," she said quietly. " And you certainly haven't done too badly as a performing dog. We live the way you said you always wanted to live. Anything we do is done the way *you* want it done. If I don't complain it's because I've been happy watching you prove things to yourself—not to other people."

He nodded grimly. " Keep going! I know the lines —I wrote them. Next comes the piece about the penniless bum with a police record that you met and married."

Brandy had dulled his mind but he knew he had gone too far. Her head was hidden, her shoulders working. He knelt at her side, stilling the shake with his arms. After a while she looked up, wet-eyed but sure of herself. " It *was* that ghastly man, wasn't it ?" she sniffed.

He hid his face in her hair the better to lie. " I dunno

23

—sometimes I think I'm going crazy, Barby!" He touched his forehead. " Policies—percentages—I live with them night and day. This business to-night finished it. I lost the guy and the account."

They did the night-time chores together. Fixing fire-guard and doorbolts—letting sweet cool air into the living room. Upstairs he lay miserable in the darkness till need sent him to her bed. They slept close through the night, her arms a buttress for him against the morning.

He left her sleeping and took an earlier train than usual. He was at Waterloo at nine. He jolted three subway stops to Trafalgar Square then walked north. A bright October sun followed the night's rain. The streets were still clean and fresh. He avoided the Haymarket—it was too near Suffolk Street and the office. He couldn't risk anyone seeing him at this hour. He used the passage by the side of the church to gain Piccadilly. Then past the shuttered tailors on Saville Row to the white façade at its end. There was a sign over a flight of steps—POLICE— it said.

Across the way was West Central Police Station. With nightfall there'd be a steady traffic up those steps. Whores, pimps and thieves—the homosexuals from the parks— their partners furtive in shame. He walked round the block and stood in a tea-bar where he could watch the street. A few pedestrians hurried along—nobody who looked like a tail. He left the bitter black brew untouched. They'd know over there what blackmail was. And the way to deal with it. He went across the street quickly. At the top of the steps he turned left. A uniformed police-man came to the counter, strangely naked without a cap. He wore sergeant's stripes and said " Sir ".

" I want to see someone from the C.I.D. office," Fraser

24

said. It came as a strange thought—never before had he been in a police station, voluntarily.

The man had his pad and pencil ready with the speed of custom. " What's the nature of your complaint, sir ?" He glanced over his shoulder at the clock on the wall. " It's a bit early for the C.I.D. Most of them don't get here much before nine-thirty."

Fraser looked at him steadily. " It's urgent and it's personal."

" I see." The cop lowered his voice. " If you wouldn't mind giving me a few particulars. May I have your name ? "

Fraser gave him one and a fictitious address to go with it.

" Take a seat, sir. I'll give C.I.D. a ring for you."

It was quiet in this big, airy room. Over at the desks by the windows, a couple of men were busy at silenced type-writers. Only the institutional clock was loud. It all came back too easily, he remembered. There'd be a place across the hallway they called the DETENTION ROOM. As long as they held you there, you weren't technically under arrest. It would be a bare, polished room without a corner for a suspect to stash a tool, a key—the scrap of paper that yelled guilt. On the far side of the room would be a second door. Made of steel, this time, and double-locked. That one would lead to the cells. Once through it there was no question of your status. You were pinched. He crossed his legs self-consciously, reminding himself which side of the fence he was on.

The cop was back to lift a flap in the counter. " Will you come this way, Mr. Bishop ? "

Fraser followed him through double glass doors, down a corridor bright with artificial light. One wall was blank.

The back of the cells, he guessed. His escort stopped out-side a door with C.I.D. painted on it. The cop opened the door shutting himself out.

This was not the main C.I.D. office. Just a small room with a barred window that gave on a well in the building. The floor no more than bare boards. Next to a coloured picture of Her Majesty hung a trench coat and a black Homburg hat. A man was studying photographs at the desk. He jerked his head at the empty chair but made no move to get up. " Sit down, Mr. Bishop! " He started stuffing tobacco into his pipe as if the gesture belonged to the occasion. He had stone-grey hair over dark, brooding eyes. Judged by his clothes alone, he belonged as readily to the exercise ring at Brixton Prison as behind a cop's desk. The shoulders of the pin-striped suit sloped a little too far. The folds of the handkerchief were too precise. " What can I do for you ? " he asked. He used no pencil or pad—only his eyes.

" A fellow who's working for me says he's being black-mailed." Fraser kept his voice impersonal. The detective used three matches on his pipe. " The man's been in jail," Fraser added. " It seems that somebody he knew there's been threatening to tell me—his friends and family —about his past. The works."

The cop's chair swivelled then pitched slightly back. " Why hasn't he come here himself ? " There was neither undue curiosity in his voice nor aggressiveness.

" Because he's scared out of his life," Fraser said hotly. " I'm his employer and I've known everything about him from the beginning. He told me. The man's a good worker and in a position of trust."

" What's his name—his address ? " The cop pulled a scribbling pad from a drawer.

26

" My business is down in Surrey—that's where we both live." Fraser kept his eyes steady. He wanted nothing from this man except verification.

" Surrey!" The cop shook his head. When he stood he seemed shorter. " There's nothing we can do here in that case, sir. You'll have to go to your local police-station."

Fraser was incredulous. " Are you kidding! Don't you *know* what a village constable's office is like ? I'm trying to help the guy—not have him run out of the neighbour-hood!"

The cop stared through the window at the blank wall. He turned suddenly. " You're an American, aren't you ? " Fraser let it pass. " Over here blackmail's something the courts know how to deal with." The man's tone was as if close contact with crime had left him indifferent to its drama. " But courts only convict on evidence, Mr. Bishop." He stopped Fraser's protest with his pipe. " Nailing a blackmailer isn't a job for amateurs—no matter how well-intentioned. I can guess what you're thinking. A man serves his time for an offence—that should finish it. And as far as we're concerned it does. Our job's the protection of the public. If an old lag happens to be part of the public—momentarily," he grinned, " He gets protection too." He opened the door to the corridor. " You seem to be a man of some substance. I suggest you see your Chief Constable. You'll find he can't do anything without the co-operation of the man involved. But he'll be ready to help."

Fraser felt the man's eyes in his back the whole length of the corridor. As he turned the corner, he heard the door shut. He passed the inquiry desk. The man nodded incuriously. Fraser took the steps to the street at a fast clip. As if the officer might yet come running after him

27

with some bawled order. Once round the block, he slack-ened speed. It was a quarter-to-ten. Plenty time. He was never in the office before half-past. That was it, then. He needed evidence. Without it the police were about as much help as a Sewing Circle—even if he decided to use them. There had been no time to think last night. Now he knew that he had to convey the menace of the building he had just left to Kline. Shock the lawyer into accep-tance of one fact—that come what may he wouldn't go through with this deal.

He crossed to Bond Street, saying his piece without sound. *I've got enough to shove you inside, Kline. Tell your story from there. If it finishes me, Okay. I'd be better digging ditches than with you round my neck.*

He stopped in front of the long display window. A printed sign read:

WE HAVE NOT ONLY THE BIGGEST BUT THE SMALLEST
AND WHATEVER WE HAVE IS THE BEST

The show of electrical appliances made the point. Giant-screen television sets, boxlike affairs for use in cars. Radios. Tape-recorders.

He had to find a means of scaring Kline. Evidence of some sort and the threat to use it.

The salesman was keen and knowledgeable. He showed Fraser the tiny wire recorder with pride. " Now the Germans really *know* how to make this sort of thing, sir." He hefted the set in the palm of his hand. " It's the smallest machine on the market. Operates on battery or mains." He touched the switch and spoke into the minute mike. Then he reversed the button. The voice was metallic but recognisable. " As you see, the mike acts as

28

speaker on the playback, sir. And here. . . ." He fitted a long cable to the set. " This is the buttonhole mike—let me show you!" He dropped the mike behind Fraser's breast-pocket handkerchief. Then he threaded the cable through Fraser's raincoat. " Fasten your belt, sir," he instructed. " Now switch on." He read rapidly from a list of gramophone records. " Notice that I can't see the set or the mike," he added. " Now play back." The re-production was faithful.

The half-hour had almost sounded when Fraser reached Suffolk Street. The tall thin house at the north end had unimpaired elegance. Net curtains draped Georgian windows and the interior was rich and polished. The upper floors were given to accountancy and general offices. The five rooms at street level formed the partners' suites and Fraser's own office. Without knowing why, he found himself tiptoeing along the edge of the hall carpet. Like a thief already, he thought. He hung his coat and hat on the rack at the end of the corridor. Two bowlers—two rolled umbrellas—were already there. He shut his door gratefully. It was a restful room with arched windows overlooking a leaf-strewn garden. It had a dark carpet, white panelling and two desks. His secretary had his personal mail waiting. She was pretty, efficient and completely sexless. He started to slit the envelopes mechanically.

Two o'clock, Jacques Bar. That crack about being quiet there was good. There'd be a crowd. Kline was bound to choose a place like that. Almost certainly the lawyer would be sitting facing the door, back to the wall. He lived by his own slogan. " Trust nobody—yourself least of all."

He hurried his way through the mail then made his

voice casual. "I'd like you to get me some files from General, Miss Donnelly!" He gave her six names. Mrs. Chester Garrett was fourth on the list. When the girl came back, he managed somehow to let the folders stay where she had put them. Five long minutes went by before he selected one. He started checking dates and figures ostentatiously against his memo pad. At the end of a quarter-hour, he'd worked down to the Garrett folder. He opened it.

Of its kind, this was a comprehensive and imposing document. The premium was high; the security measures stringent; the name of the syndicate at Lloyd's old and honoured. Attached to the policy was a copy of the Underwriters' Survey Report. Security measures had been incorporated in a sub-section of the Special Conditions Clause.

"Brick-built house fronting South Street, Mayfair. No garden or rear exit. Access to servants' quarters gained by steps to a basement with windows barred by mild-steel bars, 1" diameter. Front door has three locks. One Ingersoll, two Hobbs mortise. Two bolts and a fifteen-inch burglar chain on the inside. There are four windows facing South Street on each of three floors. The rear of the house fronts a churchyard and has three windows on each floor. All but the top floor windows are TECTATHIEF wired to West Central Police Station. Insured property normally kept in a 2 cwt. Milner wall safe in master bedroom. *Household.* Mrs. Chester Garrett, widow, no occupation. Employed persons number four, all of whom have been in Mrs. Garrett's service for more than ten years. One cook, two maids and a chauffeur."

A list of Mrs. Garrett's jewellery followed—its dimensions, origin and description. He closed the file.

Someone had scrawled " All risks " across the front and added a signature.

It was eleven when the buzzer on his desk sounded. It was his father-in-law. He dropped the files on his secretary's desk as he went out.

George Patterson was tall, with his daughter's eyes. He was alone. He walked the carpet from door to window with the restlessness of a man who has something difficult to say. He waited till Fraser was seated.

" 'Morning, Kit! I've been looking at the figures for the last quarter." Hands behind his back, he chose to aim his words at the tips of highly-polished shoes. " They're good, Kit. And most of the accounts are yours. Ridley—Field—the Garrett woman—this new thing of Pearl and Zahl's. You've worked damned hard." He halted to rub the small of his back against the jutting mantel. " You know," he continued, "next best thing to pulling off something yourself is seeing the chap you picked for the job do it!"

Fraser was uncomfortable under the older man's look. " I've had the names, sir. And a lot of luck."

" That may be," said Patterson. " You've worked at it, too. How's Barby ? "

For eleven years, Patterson had phoned his daughter every morning when she was in England. And Fraser knew it. He was suddenly cautious. " She's pretty good, I guess." He tried a grin. " You know how it is, sir. Summertime, I'm a kind of Pony Club widower. This time of the year, it's better. We get along."

Patterson nodded for his own benefit. " I want you to take a few days off, Kit. Get away with Barby somewhere. It'll do you both good."

Father and daughter were close. Watching Patterson's

31

thin face, Fraser recognised more than just friendly concern. Barby was worried and she'd told her father. Once she'd said, " I don't think I'd want to live if you weren't there, Kit." The outburst had come unprompted, unexpected. They'd been driving home at the end of a day's steeplechasing. The car open, the air in their nostrils stiff with frost. He knew she still meant it. Anything that touched his wellbeing touched hers. The scene last night had obviously disturbed her. He had to be careful.

" We've only been back from Spain a couple of months," he remarked. He had been rid of the need to lie to those near him for too long. He went back to it with resentment.

There was a tray on Patterson's desk. He opened the window to throw crumbs to the birds on the grass below. Then he closed the window carefully again. " I've been thinking a lot about you and Barby, Kit. It's easy for ambition to flag in a man of your age unless he knows just where he's going. I was the same myself." He seemed to speak freely for the first time. " Barby's mother and I always regretted not having a son, you know." He scratched his chin. " You've made up for it in many ways. What you've been doing was never meant to be a permanent job, Kit. That's partly why I want you to take Barby away for a couple of weeks." His long head punctuated his words. " There'll be something more responsible for you to do when you get back." He gave Fraser a thin, warm hand. " Sometimes a chap needs somebody to talk things over with." His smile was kind. " And I don't mean his wife! Remember you're one of the family, Kit."

Patterson's eyes were steady. Fraser avoided them. The time to tell his story to this austere old man was long since gone. Circumstances had trapped Patterson no less than himself.

He looked up, committed. " I'll have a talk with Barby to-night, sir. Thanks very much."

" You won't! You'll take your hat and get back to Two Bridges this morning," Patterson corrected. " Let us know where you are." He flicked the pages of a calendar. " I'll expect you back on the twenty-fourth." He walked Fraser to the door. " Just tell Barby whatever you think best," he said quietly.

Two weeks away from the office meant a row of cancelled appointments. It took an hour with his secretary to straighten out his engagement list. Once on the street, he used a booth to phone Barby. His brain was working coolly now, resolving the intricacies of strategy.

" A fine thing you pulled behind my back!" he joked. " I've just had a half-hour with your father. He seems to be under the impression that I'm a potential psychopath!"

She was cautious. " I haven't the first idea. . . ."

He interrupted her. " I know. You've no idea what I'm talking about. When somebody sends a message with a foghorn I get it—that's what the old man did. Guess what—I'm on two weeks' leave-of-absence. Are you surprised ? "

" Not very." She was laughing. " There's racing at Cheltenham next week. I've already called about a hotel room. Clever ? "

" Very," he said dryly. " You know, Barby, seriously— you're not the only one disturbed by last night's exhibition. I'm going to see a doctor. If the rocks in my head are shaking loose I want to know why."

She wasted no time with her answer. " I never met anyone who needed a doctor less." Her voice fenced.

" Did Daddy say anything else—about the office, I mean ? "

" He did," he said shortly. " I get promoted after the vacation. That's another reason for seeing this doctor."

" What doctor ? "

He was cunningly off-hand. " Some guy in Kensington runs a clinic for head cases. People with mild mental problems. He's supposed to have treatment that relaxes you completely in a half-dozen sessions."

She made a sound of exasperation. " The whole thing sounds completely ridiculous. *Why* should you see a doctor ?"

" This rest's your idea, remember." He was adamant. " It's probably a good one." He used the name of a doctor well-known in insurance circles. " Burns gave me the address of the clinic. A visit can do no harm."

Her voice was suddenly far away. " You do whatever you think best, darling."

" Obviously the last person I want to know about this is your father," he said. " Promise ? "

" Promise," she answered. " What do you want me to do about the hotel room. Are we going racing or not ? "

" We'll see how things work out. Look, love, I've got to dash. I'll try to be home at the usual time."

He ate an early lunch in a pub. Behind a locked door there, he experimented with the recorder. Moving the mike from door to window. Manœuvring volume till he was able to catch the traffic sounds outside—record his softest whisper. He threaded the flex carefully from mac pocket to a spot behind his breast-pocket handkerchief. Then he buttoned the mac and made the belt fast.

The bar at *Jacques* was crowded. Kline sat at one of the window tables. He raised a hand in greeting as he saw

Fraser. He climbed ponderously to his feet and came over.

" You've lunched, I hope, Kit ? Good!" He wore the same dark suit as the day before and carried a brief-case. For an absurd second Fraser imagined it holding the counterpart of his tiny recorder. Involuntarily he was staring at Kline's wrist, searching for the hidden lead.

The lawyer glanced down. " Oh *those*!" he said. He shot his cuffs showing the heavy crescent-shaped links. " I never parted with them, you see, Kit. My goodness! That really takes one back, doesn't it!" He slanted his head and laughed heartily. The girl settled his light coat round his shoulders. " Thank you, my dear!" The coin was given with graciousness.

They stood for a moment on the steps. Fraser's fingers sought the switch in the depth of his pocket. He clicked it on then off, tentatively.

" You've made up your mind, of course, Kit ?" Kline's eyes were on the passing traffic. " We need a cab," he said casually.

" A man with a gun at his head *has* no mind to make up," Fraser answered bitterly. It was an easy part to play.

Kline slowed a passing taxi. " For God's sake get the tragedy out of your voice, Kit. You're on your way to twenty thousand pounds. Not years." He gave the driver a direction. " The tea place by the bridge in Hyde Park."

The driver turned. " It's closed for the winter season, guv!"

Kline nodded. " You chaps are a mine of information," he said admiringly. " Drive us there, nevertheless," he instructed.

They stopped before the closed building, shuttered and melancholy with stacked tables and windblown leaves.

Sun had brought out the nannies and children, the dogs that raced yelping, nose to grass. Across the lake a cavalcade of small girls on outsize hacks bobbed through the trees. Kline stopped on the bridge, considering the placid water. " Lovely! " he said at last. He spat like a small boy. When the spittle hit the surface, he added, " and safe to talk in."

Beyond the Serpentine Bridge and the Magazine cars were parked. People dozed behind steering-wheels, read newspapers or stared at the passers-by. A small Jaguar had been drawn up on to the grass verge at the end of the row. Since the driver had used a litter bin as a marker, the nearest car was fifteen feet away. Kline opened one of the doors of the Jaguar. Fraser got in after him.

Over at the water's edge a man was throwing sticks for a setter. He moved easily—like a man in good condition —tall and bare-headed. When the dog raced to its owner, the man walked over to the Jaguar. He climbed behind the driving-wheel. Very blond, he was in his early thirties. He wore cavalry twill trousers and a tweed jacket. He slewed in his seat to face the two men in the back of the car.

" This is Mark Drummond, Kit," said Kline.

The blond hair was fashionably long above the ears— Drummond's face brown. " I've heard a lot about you," he said pleasantly. It was a cultured accent.

The angle at which Fraser was lolling hid the bottom half of his body from Drummond. Kline's eyes were on his partner. Fraser found the button in his pocket— flipped it without sound. He settled into his role—reluctant victim faced with his extortioners.

Kline lit a Turkish cigarette. " I don't know whether I said this before, Kit, but you two remind me so much of one another in many ways." The man in front lowered a window, wrinkling his nose at the reeking cigarettes. " Mark probably has more vision than you had, Kit," Kline said judiciously. " In fact one might say that the success of this scheme depends on Mark's expertise." He cleared his throat. " Although the germ—as it were—of the idea was mine."

Fraser chose words calculated to damage on a play-back.

" Congratulations. I always wanted to meet a black-mailer."

Drummond's face reddened. He tapped a signet ring against his teeth. " Ah well," he said at length. " I sup-pose it's understandable." He pointed over the back seat. " One thing, nevertheless—since we're going to see some-thing of one another, I suggest you adopt a more civil manner." Kline rumbled something soothing. Drum-mond waved him down. " I don't give a damn about this righteousness of yours. For me you're just an ex-thief—" He shook his head. " My conscience doesn't trouble me. That's one of the reasons I've made this business pay."

Kline blew his smoke carefully through the window. " One might add that you've had the guidance of an expert in such matters."

Drummond's face lost friendliness when he smiled. " An expert's guidance," he agreed.

Fraser shrugged. Drummond seemed bent on proving his competence. Thought of the tiny reel unwinding in Fraser's pocket was good. " Quite a guy! " His voice was level but mocking. " What do I call you—Raffles ? "

One of Kline's long arms wrapped round Fraser. The set in his pocket forgotten, Fraser tried to jerk himself free. Drummond jack-knifed his way up, hand stretched over the back of the front seat. A foot of flex dangled from the gap in Fraser's mac, dislodged by his sudden movement. He started stuffing it back mechanically. Then the weight of both men hit him simultaneously. Kline's bulk imprisoned him. Fraser gasped as Drummond's knee drove into his lower belly. He fell forward, powerless and retching. Drummond retrieved the wire recorder.

Fraser was kneeling in the well between the seats, face jammed against the car door. Thirty yards away, a man was posing a family group for a picture. One of the children's voices was shrill. Drummond's knees pinned his shoulders. He could do nothing but squat, his mouth sour with bile. Drummond's weight shifted, then he climbed into the front of the car. He had the recorder in his hands. The reel unwound. First came the sound of a car horn, squealing tyres, a dog's bark. Finally the voices of the three men. Kline's breathing sounded even more laboured than usual.

" Get up," ordered Drummond. He tossed the set to the seat beside him.

Fraser climbed up cautiously. He held his knees tight to stop them from trembling. He watched Drummond's steady hand flick a lighter. The blond passed the flame to Kline. " Do you have any more chums like this one ? " he asked the lawyer.

Kline heaved his body round to lean on Fraser. He clicked his tongue. " What did you expect to achieve by this nonsense ? I vouched for you to Mark," he complained.

Fraser concentrated. Self-control was returning slowly —it was important to hide his fear. It was no use answering Kline. He could only stall for time without knowing what time would do for him.

" I'll tell you what he expected," Drummond said easily. " One of those cinema double-crosses. With the battered hero outwitting the crooks! " He grinned. " That's it, isn't it, old man ? Trotting off to Scotland Yard with *this*," he jerked his head at the recording machine—" as evidence? " He looked at Kline sourly. " Before you start that junk about wire-recordings not being legal evidence, I'd like to ask you this. Would you be lolling back so happily if the Commissioner of Police had a record of this short conversation ? " He ripped the wire from the machine then dropped both in his pocket. " A souvenir," he said.

Fraser's forehead was cold and wet. He knew he was going to vomit. Past caring, he groped his way over Kline's legs and lurched to the shelter of a tree. When it was done he walked back to the car. Ashamed and filled with hate.

Kline shook his head. " This rather alters matters, Kit. My God," he said indignantly. " You're a copper! "

The word came back from the past. As damning as the tell-tale cross slashed across the face of a police informer. Yet it gave him hope. For surely this was the end. They could have no use for a man they didn't trust. " I told you yesterday I'd give you half the money I have, Kline," he said. " I'll make it the lot. Give me a couple of days to realise my securities and the four thousand's yours." Neither man answered. " I'll keep my word," he insisted. " Only once the money's paid, there's no more. Not a nickel! " He looked from one to the other. " If you keep at me, I'll kill you! Maybe one, maybe the other. Life won't mean enough to be blackmailed for the rest of it."

Drummond's face was impassive. He answered for

them both. " I don't *need* two thousand quid, Fraser. Nor does Kline." His blue eyes were steady. " You're not going to be foolish enough to try anything else. You've got only one chance of keeping your job—this reputation you've built up. That's with us." His voice was thin. " You'll get your share. And once it's over you'll never hear from either of us again." He shrugged. " You'll have to take my word for that! "

Fraser sought each man's eyes in turn. But he knew that the decision had been taken for him. They were partners. Till the Garrett jewellery was stolen, broken up and sold. Till he was personally twenty thousand pounds richer. He pulled a blind on the future.

" If I'm in, I'm in," he said slowly. " I'll do my part. All I ask is that it's over as quickly as possible."

Drummond shrugged. " That suits me! You know the information we want? " Fraser nodded. " How soon can you get it? " Drummond smoothed the long hair over his ears. " There's nothing you can tell me about the *outside* of the house. I've devoted over a month to Mrs. Garrett. It's the inside I'm interested in. Where's the stuff kept? " he asked suddenly.

" In a safe in her bedroom."

" I want to know its size—its serial number. What the report says about the locks on the doors, the servants. Everything."

Kline shot his cuffs, clearing his throat. He seemed happier. " You don't have to worry about Kit once he's given his word, Mark. He may be hairbrained at times but nobody knows better than Kit when it's time to get down to business. He won't give us any more trouble." Once more he wrapped an arm round Fraser in improbable comradeship.

Something was amusing Drummond. Taken by the fancy, he smiled. " I'll try to make sure that he doesn't." He leaned his chin on a hand, watching Fraser. " You're supposed to have been a good thief. I'll give you the chance to prove it. You can come in with me, old man." Wary-eyed, he added, " into the Garrett house."

He sat, shrunk and incredulous. " You must be kidding," he said after a moment. " Kline!" The lawyer was smiling too. " You're kidding," Fraser repeated half-heartedly.

Kline's full mouth curved. " I can't think why it didn't occur to me before," he said happily. " *Much* neater! All for one and one for all! "

" Cut it out," Drummond said impatiently. " Sidney Greenstreet's dead." His arm lay across the seat back. The hand was small with sensitive fingers stemming from a powerful wrist. " Can you get this information by to-morrow ? The plan I have requires action on everyone's part. You can never be sure with this woman. She's spoiled, neurotic. Ready to change her mind at the drop of a hat."

" Do you know her ?" asked Fraser.

" I know her kind," Drummond said briefly. " Well ? "

The office keys in his pocket stopped Fraser's panic. " I can get a copy of the Special Conditions clauses any time after five-thirty tonight," he answered steadily.

Drummond started the motor. " All right. You meet Kline somewhere later. Give him the stuff. How could I reach you in a hurry if I had to ? "

" That's necessary ?" asked Fraser.

" It might be."

" My number's Two Bridges 26," Fraser said. " No matter who answers the phone, your name's Dr. Landers.

You're a mental specialist who's treating me for depression."

Kline's fat laugh died under Drummond's glance. "Dr. Landers," repeated Drummond thoughtfully. "Don't worry about your wife if I have to phone. The act will be good. Do you want me to drop you somewhere?"

Fraser shook his head. "I'll meet you at six, Kline. In the buffet at Waterloo." He shut the car door.

"I'll be there, Kit." Kline's face was beaming through the rear window as the car drove off.

He started walking across the park, using the open stretches of grass in order to avoid people. It was half-past three. He'd have to call Barby again—tell her he would be late. He kept saying the name "Landers" to himself. He had a composite picture in his mind. A white-coated man with a light strapped to his forehead—wearing Drummond's smile.

He boarded an eastbound bus at the Albert Hall. The Public Library at the back of Leicester Square was quiet. A girl brought him the books he requested. Grangers' *Nervous Disorders* and the Medical Register. Landers was a name familiar in the insurance world as an expert witness in cases involving mental health. Fraser found the address. Paul Landers, Campden Hill. He leafed through the thick textbook. *Anxiety Neurosis—Lack Of Concentration.* He tried making sense of the stilted periods. It was gone quarter-past-five when he left the building. He telephoned his office. There was no reply. He found more coins and rang Two Bridges. Barby answered. He made his voice urgent. "I'm going to be late after all. I'm just on my way to see Doctor Landers. My appointment's for half-past-five. I'll try and catch the six-fifty home. O.K.?"

Her concern was the more obvious because she tried to

conceal it. " Don't let him talk you into feeling ill, Kit!"
He mumbled something reassuring. " I'll drive to the
station and pick you up," she promised.

He left the booth disturbed and thoughtful. Nobody
was closer to him than Barby. She was at once the easiest
and most dangerous person to lie to. Whatever he said she
believed without question. But she was still capable of
taking some sudden decision in order to " save him from
himself."

He walked slowly south, ready to duck in a doorway
should he run into one of the office staff. Everyone would
know that he was supposed to be home in the country. He
stopped at the corner, reconnoitring Suffolk Street. A
truck was unloading stage scenery at the back of the
theatre. A couple of men swung down the sidewalk with
the spring of the homebound. He strolled up the street.
It was at least three years since he had used his office keys.
He was fumbling at the door, feeling for the right one,
when a cracked voice sounded behind him.

" Evenin', sir." The woman was redfaced and sixty.
" I like bein' on time," she said cheerfully. " Can't abide
people wot's late!" A crazy hat bobbed on her head,
punctuating her words.

He turned the key and let her pass. Who cleaned the
offices—when—were considerations that had never concerned him. The char's bird-bright eyes watched him
intently.

" Something I forgot," he said hurriedly and shut the
office door in her face. He stood with his ear to the crack.
Pails were being rattled in the cloakroom along the
passage. Then the woman's voice started up with a thin
hopeless hymn.

If her duties took her first upstairs, he had a long wait

ahead. She must not see him up there. There were times
when his father-in-law worked late. An old biddy like this
might easily prattle. " Such a nice young man, sir, your
son-in-law. Only the other evenin' I was up in the
General Offices, doin' me cleanin'. . . . "

Even now he had some reason for being in his own
office; upstairs, none. A Hoover droned along the passage. He opened the door slightly. The char was in
Patterson's rooms, out of sight. Fraser ran up the stairs.
The two big offices were strangely unfamiliar —chairs
stacked on tables, desks tidy with precise lines of tele-
phones. He pulled a pair of gloves on. No matter how
unnecessary it seemed, he had to watch every move. The
big file doors creaked as they swung out. He pulled the
drawer labelled G. The Garrett folder was missing.
Clumsy with haste, he went through a batch of green
covers. Pulled out the other drawers. It was useless.
None of the files he had requested earlier was there. He
shut the doors with trembling hands. This panic had to be
controlled. Somehow he had to recapture the feeling of
isolation that had been his years ago. The nerveless indifference that had enabled him to stand at the side of a
sleeping woman, her jewels in his hand. He crept downstairs, eyes on the passage door. Three quick steps took
him to his office. He turned the key. The missing folders
were where he had dropped them—on his secretary's
tray. He used her typewriter, copying the vital clauses
from the Garrett policy. Finished, he wiped the roller of
the machine with a handkerchief dampened with lighter
fluid. He gained the street unseen by the woman inside.

A cab stopped at his signal. The big clock in Waterloo
Station showed two minutes to six as he pushed open the
glass door of the buffet. Kline was sitting alone at one of

the round tables. A large brief-case was in front of him. Black and with gilt initials. He ordered a drink for Fraser.

" I find something depressing about a railway station," Kline said sadly. He shrugged. " All these soldiers and sailors coming back from leave, I suppose." He frowned. " It reminds one of prison." He shook himself free of an unpleasant thought. " Well?"

Fraser slid the folded slip across the table. Kline donned heavy-framed spectacles. He might have been reading a brief. He nodded approval, snapping shut his spectacle-case. His full mouth was pursed. " A very competent report." The slip disappeared into the brief-case. " Well done, Kit! Mark will be pleased."

" Mark will be pleased," repeated Fraser. He made no effort to hide the sarcasm. He felt easier now the paper was in Kline's possession. They were one step nearer the end of it all.

Kline wagged a couple of fingers. " I don't want you to be misled by Mark's appearance," he warned. " He's a very competent young man." He smiled broadly. " If you're nervous about going into the house with him, you can forget it. Mark knows his job."

The words gave Fraser the oddest dislike. He recognised an awakened conceit of endeavour and experience. " I never scared easily," he said shortly. " I still don't." He met Kline's appraising look. " What do *you* do in all this," he asked. " Apart from being the master-mind?"

" Ah yes, that!" said Kline easily. " I sell. For cash and with complete safety." He posed both hands on the the brief-case. " In fact, the stuff's sold already." He waited till a girl went by with a tray. " All I have to do is deliver the goods."

It was probably true. That's how Kline had always worked. There were twenty walk-up offices, a hundred yards from the Diamond Bourse. In them, bright-eyed refugees with money ready for a deal. Kline had always been a two-way valve. You were never certain where the loot was sold nor the buyer where it came from. Kline's own technique in stripping a stone from its setting bordered on the professional.

" Still doing business at the old stand," he wondered.

" The less you bother yourself with such matters, the less reason you'll have to worry," Kline said quietly. " You seem to have developed a tendency to worry. It's important that you don't. How do you get along with that long-legged wife of yours ?"

To hear Kline even talk of Barby was distasteful. " Let's keep my wife out of it," he said shortly. " None of this has got to touch her. Is that understood ? "

Kline sighed, leaning forward as if unfolding wings for flight. " *Anything* a man does touches the woman he lives with. As I know to my sorrow, Kit. If you're not acting normally your wife will start wondering why. And a wondering wife's a danger. I meant to mention this before. You've got to behave normally—at home and at your office. Not only before the job but when it's over." The heavy-lidded eyes were steady. There was no mockery in Kline's voice.

" Behave normally ! " Fraser said. " You don't remember what it *is* to behave normally, Kline." He shook his head. " Otherwise you couldn't say a thing like that ! I've got two weeks away from the office. If you think my wife won't notice anything unusual, you're crazy. That's why she's got to think I'm getting psychiatric treatment."

Kline was suddenly solicitous. "There isn't any question of you really being ill, is there?"

Fraser took a look through the window. The big hand of the clock covered the quarter-hour. "I never felt better in my life." He grinned. "I've got five minutes to catch my train."

Kline got to his feet. "I'm afraid we're going to have to meet again tomorrow, Kit. Let's say same place, same time—*Jacques*. And Kit—" He pushed a slip of paper into Fraser's hand. "You read this phone number backwards —dial the last digit first. The exchange is easy to remember. If you're ever in trouble, this number will get me."

"If I'm ever in trouble," Fraser repeated. The two men smiled at one another. "Goodbye Kline," he said.

Barby was waiting at the station. Seeing her at the barrier was a return to the first days of their marriage. Every morning she had driven him to the station in the small green convertible. With the first hard frosts, he had encouraged her to sleep on. The acquisition of the Buick had left her content to let him drive.

They crossed the station yard arm-in-arm. Here it was peaceful after the violence of the day. Dusk with a few lights burning in the farms on the wooded slopes. The pungent smell of burning leaves—an involuntary memory taking him back to the house in the Humber Valley that had been home.

He took the driveway fast as usual. Ready with a detailed description of his interview with the doctor. Barby was determined to talk about anything else. The rascality of a timber merchant who'd sent wet logs—a pony gone lame. Kate Gilmour. "She was in tears when she

47

phoned," said Barby. " It seems it's *every* night now! Jim comes back from town sober enough. But an hour later, he's stinking. Their maid's given notice."

The triteness of the tale irritated him. What did these people know of trouble! " Living with Kate would drive me to drink too," he said sourly. He and Barby had never made any play for popularity in the neighbourhood. They did none of the right things. Barby had her Pony Club—that was half her life. For him, all it meant was a few snub-nosed children at the tea-table a couple of times a month. He knew few of the parents. Barby and he weren't members of the country club. They avoided the Sunday morning gin sessions at the *Dog and Fox* and re-fused to subscribe to the local Conservative Association. It had always been more fun to avoid these week-end farmers, desperately knowledgeable about prize Jerseys. Less perceptive about their loud-voiced and sex-starved women who spiced their drinks with scandal.

He rolled the garage door down. Barby had snapped the light in the kitchen. Even she had this preoccupation with other people's affairs, he thought. Kate Gilmour and her husband for instance.

It was no more than nine when he said he was ready for bed. Barby was willing. They lay in the darkness, not speaking, listening to the bedside radio. He switched off the set on an impulse.

" I've been happy these past years, Barby," he said slowly. " It couldn't have been the same without you—with anyone else."

He heard her stir lazily. Her voice was husky. " When you *do* manage to say something nice, darling, it's the best ever." She was settling for the night. He didn't have to see her with his eyes. A hundred times he'd watched her

sleeping. She'd be curled with her knees close to her chin
—her nose just peeping from the sheets. She sighed deeply.
" I'm terrible, Kit. I feel desperately sorry for Kate Gilmour—but I can't help feeling smug when I think of us.
You know ? "

He was propped on his elbow, staring at her bed. He
fancied that he could see the curve of her face in the tiny
glow from the travel clock. " Goodnight, my darling,"
he said quietly. He pulled the pillow over his face so that
the darkness was complete.

They ate their breakfast in the little sun room. The
east wall was glass, the furnishing functional—a low table,
a rack of magazines and cane chairs. He had awakened
early to unending consideration of the past thirty-six
hours. He had no appetite, toying with his meal, parry-
ing the questions Barby produced with determined dis-
interest.

The phone rang in the living-room. She went to
answer it, carrying the breakfast tray with her. He
polished the tip of one shoe moodily. The little food he
had eaten left a queasy lump in his stomach. His mouth
tasted of tarnished metal. It was impossible to hear what
she was saying on the phone. But he had a lie ready for
her when she came back. Any call now might be from
Drummond.

Not a worry in the world, he thought, looking at her.
She wore a green jersey dress and carried a cashmere coat
on her arm. Vigorous brushing had left highlights in her
copper hair. " It was Daddy," she said. " We're going to
lunch together." She shifted the bowl of striped fish into
the shade. " What are you doing ? "

He didn't like what was happening. He was becoming
suspicious of the most innocently-framed questions. The

49

readiness to spy on her was destroying the mutual trust they had always had.

" I must know, darling," she said patiently. " Because of lunch. If you're going to be here, I'll have to leave word for Mrs. Ellis."

He got to his feet. " I'm driving up to town. It looks as though I'm going to have to see the doctor every day."

" Then I'll come up with you," she decided. " I can do some shopping this morning—go to Mummy for tea. Is he nice, this Doctor Landers?" Her tone was far too casual.

He lowered the shades to cut the wintry sun from the room. " I don't know whether he's nice. What matters is that he's good."

" You still haven't told me what he says is wrong with you," she pointed out.

He sprinkled fish food into the bowl. " I'm suffering from an anxiety neurosis," he said calmly. He went ahead of her down the corridor.

Her heels tapped as she hurried to catch up with him. " And what does he say is the remedy?"

He stopped, one hand on the living-room door. " He doesn't—not yet. First you have to find out what *creates* an anxiety neurosis. That can take time!"

While she was upstairs, he slipped into the living-room and poured himself a shot from the brandy decanter. It killed the uneasiness in his stomach. Yet he'd have to watch this running to the bottle every five minutes. This past couple of days, the trips were too often.

It was past ten when he manœuvred the Buick to the kerb behind Harrods. Barby swivelled the driving-mirror and touched red to her mouth. He leaned across and kissed her cheek. It was clear and free of make-up.

" I'll pick you up at your mother's about five," he promised. He watched her go, long-legged and as always slightly off-balance. She turned to wave from the door. He touched the horn in answer and wheeled the car east.

At Knightsbridge he cut into the park to halt at the end of the South Carriage Way. Past the trees and bushes marking the park's limits, the tops of buses were moving in slow procession. To the left was the white pile of the Dorchester Hotel and the balcony of the place where Barby had her hair done. Beyond these, South Street and the Garrett house. He'd been there just once. Six months before when he'd taken the policy for signature. The memory was hardly reassuring.

Kline and Drummond seemed happy to suppose that the security precautions there had been taken at the under-writers' insistence. They couldn't be more wrong. Elizabeth Garrett had outlived two husbands—both wealthy. For twenty-five years, the gossip writers had reported her activities, occasionally with accuracy. He saw her as she had been at the interview. Ash blonde, slim. In spite of her age still attractive. She had the modified accent of the American long in England. She told him of the seven attempts over the years to rob her. Four had been successful. For a year her jewellery had stayed in a vault. Last January she called in an expert on burglary prevention. Bolts, bars and alarms were to his design. The under-writers' surveyor had no more than approved them.

She'd signed the proposal form, her voice firm. " The premiums I'm asked to pay these days are exorbitant, Mr. Fraser. I may be a much-robbed woman. I'm still a cautious one. If it happens again, I want to be sure of the company I'm dealing with. Have your man look the house over—if he says we need more locks, we'll get them."

51

His impression had been that there wasn't a thief in London capable of beating the house without inside information. Her servants were both well-paid and loyal. For a burglar it seemed a hopeless proposition. The house was never left empty. Mrs. Garrett's jewellery stayed either on her neck, arms or ears or in the safe in her bedroom.

He pitched the half-burned stub through the car window. The Mayfair mile was the mecca of every screwsman in town. From the plausible operators who made it their home, to the spivs from the suburbs with no more than hope and a jemmy on their side. From Bond Street west to Park Lane, Piccadilly north to Oxford Street, the cops' beats were less predictable. Flying Squad cars cruised there more frequently. Every doorman and servant in the area knew what to do, faced with the unusual or suspicious. A call to 999 would have the block surrounded.

He started the motor and moved into the eastbound stream of traffic. One thing mattered now. Success. Anything short of it meant disgrace—either in or out of prison. He crossed Park Street into a mews where chauffeurs were washing their cars. He locked up and walked to South Street. As he turned the corner he slowed. It was like riding a bicycle, he thought. You never forgot entirely. Expertise was only part of successful burglary. Your mind had to work differently from that of the layman. Accepting and rejecting symbols of safety and danger automatically.

He walked across the street to the Garrett house side. He knew the picture he made. Brown polished brogues and grey flannel suit. Ordinary and respectable. He swung his car keys from a finger with the assurance of a man about his lawful occasions. On appearance alone, there wasn't a cop who'd give him a second glance. He looked cautiously at the white-painted house. A sun blind had been lowered over the front door. The brass surrounds of three locks glittered. The lower windows were down six inches. An apparent invitation to the first prowler with the nerve to step from doorstep to window sill. Once the guy had broken the beam, it would take minutes to have the street swarming with cops.

He propped a foot on the railings at the top of the basement steps. Re-tying a shoelace, he inspected the barred windows in the area. The door down there was open. Next to the garbage can was a dog's drinking bowl. He straightened up and walked on. He'd seen no dog when he'd been to the house—there had been no mention of one in the insurance policy. Either it had been overlooked or the dog had been bought within the last six months.

He went back to the car and sat with a cigarette. Without a continuous watch on the house, there was no safe way of determining the dog's size. The old gag—the call from "The League for Canine Defence" would never go unchecked in that household. Great Dane or Peke, just one yip could ruin the most careful planning. Drummond had to be told immediately.

Outside, the shirt-sleeved men were still swabbing their cars. With the first police whistle people like that would go charging up the mews, ready to trip, stun or chase a fugitive. It was less a case of guarding other's property than lust in the hunt. There wasn't a man born who didn't respond to the chase of his fellow.

With the thought of creeping into that house at night, he felt sick again. Opening locked doors, facing the unknown quantity behind them. He drove from the mews, towards South Street. At the corner he braked suddenly.

A Bentley moved to a silent stop in front of the Garrett house. The chauffeur ran down the basement steps. Fraser pulled some maps from the glove compartment and pretended to read them. He was fifty yards from the house.

He waited the space of two nervously-smoked cigarettes. The man reappeared through the front door. He was carrying a mink coat and leading a long-haired Dachshund. Mrs. Garrett followed. A maid waited at the street door till mistress and dog were settled in the back of the car. When the Bentley passed, Fraser bent double.

He ate, then found an empty space in St. James's Square. Leaving his car, he walked north to *Jacques*. By the clock over the bar he was early. The room was crowded. He worked his way through the packed clamour at the bar and back to the entrance. There was no sign of Kline.

A couple of tables behind him were littered with magazines. He took a seat, leafing the glossy pages. In front of him steps led down to the cloakrooms. He watched incuriously as a tall man climbed them unhurriedly. Then suddenly he had the certainty the man was going to speak to him.

The stranger had a farmer's red face and wore tweeds. His brusque voice was out of keeping with the rest of his appearance. " Mr. Fraser? " he asked. Uninvited, he took the seat next to Fraser. He dropped his raglan coat across his knees. A small folder peeped from his fingers. " Detective-Sergeant Bannon," he said quietly. " I wonder if you'd mind coming with me, Mr. Fraser." It was at once a request and an order. He pocketed the warrant card.

Fraser tensed, shifting his weight. The open street was a dozen steps away. Outside, the rush of early afternoon traffic. If he went now, he could sprint the length of Princes Arcade to freedom.

Bannon was watching him. " That isn't going to be necessary, I don't think. I'm not going to take more than ten minutes of your time." He stood waiting as Fraser looked up, uncertain. " You don't even *have* to come, sir. But I suggest you'd be saving yourself a great deal of bother if you did."

He wore an old-fashioned watch-chain and a sprig of heather in his lapel. He jerked his head at the door. " There's a pub round the corner where we can talk quietly. I'll wait for you there."

Fraser stayed where he was. Nobody else in the bar had given the detective a second glance. It was still only five minutes to two. He walked to the glass door and out to the street. Beyond the corner was a hanging sign. WINE BY THE GLASS. On impulse he hurried back to *Jacques* and left a message.

Bannon was waiting in the wine bar. Two slim glasses of sherry were on the table. " Leave it if you don't like it, sir. At least it gives us an excuse to sit." He started feeding shag tobacco into a rolling machine. As he licked the gummed edge, he looked at Fraser curiously. " I won't waste any time, Mr. Fraser," he said. " You know a Kline—a Mr. Maximilian Kline." He lit the crumpled cylinder. He seemed indifferent to Fraser's answer— intent on warding off the burning shreds of tobacco that fell from his cigarette.

Fraser watched him warily. For the moment he was less afraid than unsure. " Before I'm going to answer any of your questions," he said easily, " you're going to have to tell me what this is all about. You're a policeman. O.K. What's your business with me ? "

Bannon leaned back, creaking the seat. He was playing with the heavy silver watch-chain. " Fair enough, Mr. Fraser. I won't beat about the bush." He lowered his voice. " The Kline I mean represented you eight years ago when you appeared on trial at the Old Bailey. We're talking about the same man, aren't we, sir ? "

The bar was suddenly quiet. He could hear the snuffling of the watery-eyed man sitting across the room. Fraser touched the sherry to his mouth. He made no answer—just stared at the detective.

Bannon cleared his throat. His voice was patient—almost gentle. " You take my word for it, mister. If we'd had any other way of getting hold of you without up-setting your family—your employer—we'd have used it." He leant both forearms on the table and pushed his head near enough for Fraser to see the dried soap under one ear. " I'm not trying to trick you or cause you trouble." The stained soggy butt bounced in his mouth as he talked. " You know we keep an eye on our old customers—the ones that make good as well as the repeaters. I know a lot about you, Mr. Fraser. Most of it to your credit." He rolled the cheap sherry on his tongue as if it were vintage. " In the insurance business now, aren't you, sir ? "

He would have run had there been some place to run to. He made his answer mechanically, sure that his guilt must show in every gesture. " I'm in the insurance business," he agreed.

Bannon flicked an inch of ash to the floor. " Kline's been inside himself since your day—did you know that ? "

" You keep saying Kline," Fraser said edgily. " That's the third or fourth time you've mentioned his name. Let's have it—what's Kline got to do with you dragging me in here ? "

"A fair question *if* you don't already know," Bannon answered. His face lost some of its amiability. "You meet all kinds on this job. Personally, I never met a black-mailer worth more than a rope round his neck. That's what Kline went inside for, you know. Jail taught him nothing. Since he's been out, he's ruined a couple of people. Both of them chaps like you. Fellows trying to make good with a prison record to hide."

Fraser was wary. In spite of Bannon's precise infor-mation, how could he have known of this meeting with Kline. Nobody had known but the lawyer and Fraser himself. Fraser shrugged. "You still haven't said why you associate me with Kline now—unless you suspect me of blackmail too?"

Bannon shook his head. "I don't think you believe that yourself. You listen to me, Mr. Fraser. When I said this man has ruined a couple of chaps like yourself, I meant just that. The only reason he's walking the streets a free man is because neither of those chaps had the guts to give us the evidence to nail him!"

Fraser concentrated on the bottles behind the bar. Uppermost in his mind was relief. It was all over—that's what mattered. There could be no robbery now. Not with the law one short grab behind Kline's collar. Yet the conspiracy still had to be protected.

He found frankness—a smile. "You're the first human cop I ever met, Sergeant. And I've been on the level with you. You'll have to be more explicit! Everything you say's probably true but it doesn't affect me! I've seen Kline twice in eight years. Both times more or less by accident."

Bannon used spectacles as he consulted a notebook dredged from a pocket. "The day before yesterday—"

he peered over the frames—" Kline took the same train as you did to Two Bridges. He telephoned your house from the *Dog and Fox* in the village. About an hour later you drove him to the station in your car." He dropped the notebook back in his pocket—slapped his side as though turning a key on the evidence. " If that was one of the occasions you mean, you'll have to admit it doesn't look any too casual! "

" That's great," Fraser said sarcastically. " I didn't know you carried your check on old customers *that* far. It'll make quite a story for my neighbours. And they'll hear that the London police have been snooping round after me. You can't kill a story like that in a village as small as ours." He pushed the half-empty glass across the table. " There must be someone in authority who'll be interested to hear about Metropolitan Police procedure."

" *Nobody* knows anything in Two Bridges," Bannon said calmly. He added. " If you could get it into your head that we're *with* you, not against you, it would be easier, Mr. Fraser."

" *With* me! " said Fraser, half-up from his chair. " You listen to me! Then go back and report to whoever gives you your orders. Kline came to Two Bridges to ask me for money. When you stopped me to-day, I was on my way to give it to him. Not because he threatened me, sergeant. It isn't easy to refuse when you've known a man well." He checked with his watch. It was twenty-past two. " In a couple of minutes, I'll be giving him the money he asked for. For the first and the last time. Now as far as I'm concerned that winds up this interview."

Bannon's hand stayed Fraser. " You're in the insurance business," said the detective. " You've got access to information Kline could use. We have reason for thinking that he's capable of threats to obtain it."

Fraser removed the cop's hand. The watery-eyed drunk at the bar turned and was watching them with tottering interest. Fraser kept his voice down. " I'm past blackmail, Bannon. I've got nothing to hide and nothing to fear! "

The detective shrugged into his raglan. " I'm glad to hear it. That makes it easy for you to help us. When Kline *does* threaten you, the law's on your side. Perhaps you'll remember that, sir ? "

Another five minutes had passed. Kline would be getting impatient by now. It was pleasant to conjecture how good the lawyer would be on the receiving end of a shock. " I said you're the first human cop I'd met," he said steadily. " I still think so. But you're wasting your time." The drunk was teetering curiously. Fraser stared him down. " I don't intend to say anything to Kline about this meeting. You see, I'll never see him again after today," he said steadily. " I wouldn't even know where to find him."

Bannon's eyes were inscrutable. " He'll know where to find you. When he does, perhaps you'll give this number a ring." He pushed a piece of paper at Fraser. " If I'm not there, a message will reach me within the hour." He stood, fastening his coat. " Good luck, Mr. Fraser and good-bye."

Ducking into the heavy traffic, Fraser ran up the steps to the restaurant. Kline was not there. Nor did the barmen or waiters remember having seen him. Waited and gone, thought Fraser. Kline was probably at home by now. Sitting in front of his phone like an indignant vulture. He stood for a while at the top of the steps then walked slowly west to Duke Street. Once round the corner, he broke into a run that took him to the side entrance of Fortnum and Mason. There he crossed the hall to the florist shop. He watched both entrances while the girl pulled a carnation through his buttonhole. There was no sign of Bannon.

He went across the hall and called Kline's number. Someone took the call on the second buzz. Fraser wasted no time. " Kline ? I've got to see you right away."

The lawyer's voice was brusque. " I waited twenty minutes. What happened to you ? "

" Save it," said Fraser. " Just tell me how soon we can meet. When I say it's important for all of us, that's exactly what I mean." There was no stir from the other end of the line. " Are you listening, Kline ? This is bad ! "

Kline was irritated. " Relax, for God's sake ! You sound like an agitated housemaid in the family way. Where are you now ? "

Fraser grinned to himself. It would be interesting to see how much of Kline's sarcasm was left when he heard the news.

" Piccadilly," he said.

" You know Pont Street ? " Kline's voice took on the reluctant patience people use with somebody else's child.

" Number four hundred. It's a block of flats called Tower Lodge. Use the servants' entrance at the end of the building. Walk up two flights and go through the pass door to the corridor. Number thirty-nine's the first flat to your right. I'll be waiting. And take a cab ! "

He paid off the taxi at the corner of Pont Street and Sloane Street then walked a block west. The apartment building was imposing in grey freestone. Passing the main entrance, he caught a glimpse of marble and uniforms.

There was even a fountain playing in front of the heavy glass doors. Evidently extortion paid good dividends.

At the back a concrete driveway sloped down to residents' garages. He went through a door marked TRADESMEN. A bare stone staircase was beyond. He climbed to the second storey pass-door and went through to the corridor. It was hushed there—warm and dimly-lit. Outside thirty-nine he stopped. There were two Bramah locks on the door. One at chest, the other at knee level. The toughest locks in the business, he thought. Unauthorised visitors to this flat would need both time and ingenuity.

As he pressed the button, chimes sounded inside. Then the door opened. Kline beckoned him in. He stood for a moment at the barely-opened door, listening. Satisfied, he shut the door with his rump. He was wearing a big meaningless smile. " Come in," he invited. He led the way to a bright living-room. Impressionist prints framed in white wood were on the walls. A spinet was used as a desk. Behind the drinks-trolly was a second door, closed.

Kline had dressed in opulent mood. Brown suit, tie and shoes blended perfectly. " Now sit down, Kit," he said easily. " Drink ? "

The setting was pleasant. The sun shone through wide windows on pale-blue walls and carpet. Nothing was missing, thought Fraser. Down to the picture of the middle-aged woman on top of the spinet.

Kline caught his eye. " My wife," he said sadly. " I regret that she's not here to receive you. We've been separated for five years." He shook his head and busied himself with the whisky bottle. He poured, looking at Fraser for guidance. When he had splashed soda and added ice, he handed Fraser the glass. He sat poised, holding his own drink high like a chalice. " What's the trouble, Kit ? " he said quietly.

" The worst kind," said Fraser with satisfaction. " Police. That's what made me late. Have you ever heard of a man at the Yard called Bannon ? "

" Bannon ? " Kline frowned, searching the bottom of his glass as though the answer might be written there. " No," he said finally. He was showing no anxiety.

" Well, he knows you," Fraser said shortly. " *And* me." Kline's eyes never left Fraser's face. " If we go on with this Garrett thing," continued Fraser. " We all land inside." He set the glass down carefully. Walking from chair to window, he recounted the interview with Bannon. Nothing was added—nothing missed.

Kline sat through the recital, a brooding hulk. Watching intently as he listened. When he had said his piece, Fraser stood at the open window. Kline was taking this badly. It was in the big man's sudden lack of words—his drooping head. Kline was breathing hard. " We're back to what I offered in the first place, Kline. Two thousand quid. I can't be sure about Drummond. But you're certainly washed up around here." He crossed to stand over the lawyer. Near enough to see the man's clean, greased scalp. " You know what I'd do in your place," he said softly. " I'd take my money and put as much space between me and England as I could. And I'd do it quickly. You're not popular at the Yard, Kline ! "

The lawyer lifted his head to show dark amused eyes. " I don't think that's going to be necessary," he said mildly. " Though I can well understand your enthusiasm. I'm afraid you'll either have to curb or divert it." Fraser stood, uncertain. Reaching up lazily, Kline rapped on the bedroom door behind him.

It opened. The cop Bannon came into the room. He dropped a package of tobacco, roller, silver watch-chain, into Kline's lap as he passed. " The props," he grinned. He touched the heather in his lapel. " I'll keep this. For luck." Fraser had sat down. Bannon came over. " Always make them *open* their warrant cards, old boy," he advised. He flipped the folder with a thumb. Inside was a printed card.

COMPLIMENTARY PASS
WHITE CITY STADIUM

Fraser was unable to think properly. The two men's voices sounded in the hall behind. Kline was saying good-bye. Then the door closed. As he looked up, the lawyer's face was distorted with laughter in the gilt mirror.

" I'm sorry about that, Kit. Of course he's not a detective. Just an actor who used to be a client. He owes me a favour, Kit. There's nothing to worry about. He knows nothing of our plan."

He lowered himself into his chair. " I never mistrusted your intentions, Kit. Only your ability to stand pressure. One has to be certain when the stakes are big." He finished his glass, crossed his legs and continued. " The honest life's apt to make a man go soft. There were three things you might have done," he said reflectively. He might have been considering a principle of deep moral significance. " Told Bannon that you were ready to co-operate. Perhaps you might have phoned that number he gave you! " He started to laugh then choked. After a moment he sat up straight and wiped his streaming eyes.

"The Temperance Billiard Hall!" he gasped. He apologized, composing his face with an effort. "Or you could have listened to what Bannon said and told me nothing." He wagged a finger. "That's as dangerous as the first. Or do what you did. Now I know we're safe with you, Kit!"

One day, he knew, he'd sink his thumbs deep in the swelling throat. Choke till terror replaced amusement in Kline's eyes. "You're sure you have no more surprises?" he asked unevenly. "No more tricks that need an audience?"

Kline shook his cuffs free at the wrists. "Nothing, Kit. You're a full-time partner on a full-time basis."

"Just what was that in aid of—the *Jacques Bar* at two deal?"

"Just a place where you could be picked up conveniently. Nothing more," said Kline easily.

Fraser twisted in his chair. "O.K. Now I have a little news for you. And this is no theatrical performance." He used each word like a brick hurled at the other. "There's a dog in the Garrett house. A dachshund. At two or three in the morning, it should make our job real interesting."

Kline's nose narrowed. He cocked his head as if listening. "A dog! You said nothing about it before. Why wasn't it mentioned on the paper you gave me?"

"Who the hell knows!" said Fraser. "What matters is that I've seen it. You better get this straight, Kline. If I'm in on this job, I'm going to be as sure as I can that we pull it off. I'll check every detail independently of Raffles. Just tell him that! Tell him there's a cute little brown dog that probably sleeps on her bed. Maybe *he'll* know what to do about it."

Downstairs, he waited at the exit for a while. Nothing was beyond suspicion. The black laundry van across the street. The man in the doorway with his bicycle clips and gladstone bag. Even the half-open door to the church vestry. He had the feeling of being involved in some desperate game in which his opponents changed side, ad libbing the rules at will.

Kline's windows overlooked Pont Street. Sooner than pass in front of them Fraser circled the block to reach a cab. It was four-thirty when he arrived at the backwater between the Royal Mews and Victoria Street. The short cul-de-sac had a row of Queen Anne houses along one side. Brass plates plastered eleven doors, bearing the names of consulting engineers, architects. Only the last house showed signs of being really lived in. Street door and window frames were painted yellow—a cat dozed in front of a tubbed shrub.

He rang the doorbell. It was answered immediately by a maid wearing old-fashioned cap and apron. She had thin carroty hair and contempt for those neither born nor bred Scots.

" They're up in the drawing-room," she said dourly and left him to find his way.

The hall had the old familiar smell of mixed roses and beeswax. Steel engravings of Calvinistic priest-warriors hung precisely along the panelling. A small wooden shield by the door to the cloakroom. Under it, in Gaelic, the motto: ALWAYS WITH HONOUR.

He went into the cloakroom. Somehow, he had never felt at home in this house. Everything irritated him. The sense of order—the smell of pine soap. The chilly radiators that were never turned on before 1st November. When he had washed his hands, he ran water on his hair and

65

combed it tidy. He stood outside the drawing-room for a moment, then rapped and went in.

The room was long with tables and a couch in front of the windows. Tallboys gleamed with polished age, reflecting Jacobean silver. His mother-in-law sat with her back to the light, facing her tea-trolly as a pilot does his controls. Even before he bent to kiss her cheek, Helen Patterson had started to pour his tea.

" For once you're early, Kit," she said. Her hair was painstakingly groomed and very white over violet eyes. She smiled up at him, holding her chin like a woman conscious of an unkind neckline. She took a cigarette from her case, moving her hands with speed yet grace. " What *is* all this nonsense Barby's just been telling me ? " she asked.

He looked cautiously at the pair on the sofa. Patterson made room for him. As Fraser sat down, he felt Barby's hand take his, grip it tight.

" Mother's surprised we're going to spend this couple of weeks at Two Bridges," said Barby.

He shrugged, holding the shallow cup of China tea carefully.

" Why not ? "

" Both of you must be slightly mad," decided Mrs. Patterson. " Only today I read in the Times that it's seventy-five degrees in Malaga, with brilliant sunshine."

Patterson explored the inside of his stiff white collar.

" I don't know, Helen. They've already been to Spain once this year. Personally, Two Bridges at this time of the year sounds delightful. The woods—" He hesitated then ran out of words.

His wife's shoulders lifted. Her clear voice carried.

" The woods! " she scoffed. " Sloshing about in gum-boots and macintoshes. You're in your bed for a week after two days of it! "

" Anyway *we* like it," said Barby firmly. " And we're going to the races at Cheltenham next week."

Fraser left the tea untouched. Here they all sat, one slight shove from disgrace and disaster, arguing the pro-priety of spending a fortnight in the country. If he told them the truth only Barby would have the slightest idea what he meant. Words like " blackmail ", " ex-convict " —the situations they connoted—were beyond their ex-perience. Patterson's knowledge of crime came from *Stone's Justices' Manual*—his wife's from the Sunday newspapers.

He looked from one to the other. " I can relax at Two Bridges," he said steadily. " That's what I need."

Patterson put an arm round his daughter, winking at Fraser. " Good God, Helen, you make Two Bridges sound like a jail."

He couldn't even manage a smile. This ghastly con-spiracy had each of them concealing something from the others. Paired them off, in confused loyalty. He and Barby. Barby and her father. Patterson and his wife. And he alone knowing how near the end they all were. He looked at his watch. " O.K., darling. It's after five. Let's try to beat the Rat Race home."

Downstairs, Patterson followed him into the cloakroom. He stood behind Fraser, holding the gaberdine storm-coat. " I want you to take this, Kit," Patterson said suddenly. The blue cheque form he held was on Patterson's private bank. Fraser could see the figures on it—one hundred pounds. He made no move.

Patterson pushed the cheque into one of the big coat

pockets. " You're going to need a little extra." His eyes were kindly.

" I don't need it, sir," Fraser said obstinately. " I promise you."

Patterson set his back against the door. " Then use it to buy a new set of tyres for that monstrous car of yours," he said doggedly. He lowered his voice. " I probably sounded terribly pompous the other day, Kit. I just wanted you to know that I'm there when you want me." He peered, a little short-sighted, into Fraser's face.

Fraser knew that Barby had talked again. Patterson was no actor, especially when his emotions were aroused. Tired of the ludicrous masculine conspiracy, he answered wearily. " I'll remember, sir. Only right now there's nothing to discuss."

The two women's voices were loud in the hall. He shifted uncomfortably. The tiny room was suddenly oppressive. Patterson nodded a couple of times then let his breath go. " I know, Kit," he said uncertainly. " You're a good chap. And good to Barby. We're a family, Kit. That's what matters." He opened the door and led the way into the hall.

The beech trees beyond Two Bridges station were the colour of new pennies in the last of the sun. At the turn to the house, he braked hard, steering the car with exaggerated care. Afraid of what might be waiting once he rounded the last sweep of the firs. He felt Barby's weight shift as the car crunched slowly over the gravel. Without looking at her, he knew she was watching him. Hiding his terror from her was hardest of all.

He stopped the car in front of the house. Smoke from the chimneys drifted into the falling twilight. A crow flapped from the lawn, croaking warning. Smaller birds followed sending the dangling coconut shell swinging like a pendulum. It was home. Always he'd been safe here—hidden. The dark tall trees stood like lookouts barring the way from the road. He was barely conscious that Barby had gone into the house. She came back to touch his shoulder gently through the open car window. He looked up at her, startled.

She was smiling. " You're not proposing to spend the night there, are you, darling ? "

He drove round to the garage. Lights came on, cutting the shadows, as Barby busied herself upstairs. In the living-room he pulled the shades, shutting out the night. He looked for the key to the desk drawer—locked Patterson's cheque in the small steel box. Then he saw the message propped against the framed portrait of Barby.

MR. FRASER. Dr. Landers has phoned twice
this afternoon, sir. He says will you phone this
number soon as you are back.

The number was Kline's. He felt the sudden warmth of Barby's body as she leaned over him from behind. She touched his ear with first her lips then her teeth. She read the message aloud over his shoulder.

" My God ! You must be the man's first case in years ! " Her voice was unsteady.

He pulled her down brusquely to the arm-rest. Her nervous smile vanished as she met his look. " Daddy's little girl ! " he said accusingly. " You couldn't wait to tell your father I was seeing a doctor, could you ! How come you left your mother out of the act ? "

She freed her arm from his fingers, rubbing bruised flesh. " I told him," she said defiantly. She was suddenly pleading. " You can't go on like this, bottling things up, darling. You've got to talk about whatever it is that's worrying you. You won't talk to me. I thought a man might be different. Somebody you can trust. You don't seem to trust me any more," she finished sadly.

He made no answer. She pulled his head to her breast with one swift movement. " *Tell* me! " she pleaded.

He broke her hold to turn the key in the drawer. He pushed Patterson's cheque at her. " I've *got* a man to talk to," he said. " The doctor. Give this back to your father. Tell him what you like but keep him out of my hair." He controlled his voice with an effort.

" You were the ones who decided I needed a rest," he said. " It turns out you were right. Now Landers is the only one who can help me." He hauled himself from his seat and stood looking down at her. Then he put his mouth on hers. " It isn't that I don't trust you, Barby," he said with difficulty. " Just don't ask for explanations till I'm finished with the doctor." He walked over to the fireplace and knelt, putting a light to the wood. He looked up at her. " A hundred times you've said it. 'A woman will do anything for the man she loves.' O.K. It's little enough I'm asking you—some of this trust you've been talking about."

She was folding the cheque over and over. " All right," she said at last. " All right, Kit. All I ask is that nothing comes between us. Just that, nothing else." Chin high, she went out to the kitchen.

When he heard the sound of running water, he crept upstairs, the scrap of paper in his hand. He made the call, cupping the mouthpiece as though surrounded by eaves-droppers.

Kline answered. " Dr. Landers, please," Fraser said

softly. Drummond's voice was quiet, discreet. " Good evening, Mr. Fraser. There's no cause for alarm. It's just that the tests we did today were inconclusive. I'd like you here tomorrow at eleven. Here at the clinic," he added meaningly.

" I'll be there." Fraser put the phone down gingerly. There was a tinkle from the extension downstairs. Then he went into the bathroom and washed noisily. After dinner, they sat in front of the fire. He watched every move she made with caution. The silent television set—the decanter and glass by his side—-the warm friendly room. Invitation to confidence, he thought grimly. They were in bed before the cracked bell from the village sounded ten.

Waking now was a throwback to early mornings at his first prep school—a scared peek at a day that could hold no good. Barby's head was dark against the sheets in the half-light. She was still sleeping as he left the heavy warmth of the bedroom and tip-toed downstairs. She'd go on sleeping undisturbed by the familiar sounds of the morning chores.

He raked ash and cinders from the furnace—opened doors and windows. Treading across the brick-paved yard in his slippers, he carried the bucket of ashes to the garbage pail. Grey grit hissed as it hit kitchen refuse. He clamped the heavy cover in place and stood uncertain whether or not to wake Barby.

There was no strength yet in the morning sun. Mist like candy floss spread down the hill from the reservoir, muffling the toll of the village bell. House and trees were an island in an opaque sea. Over his head, three crows sat on the power-line, silent and watchful. Next year, come spring and seed grass growing on the lawn, he'd have to do something about the crows. He clung to the thought *next year*.

He lifted the door to the garage. It was warm in there with the hot reek of a kerosene stove. The car would start easily. He could be through the trees and on to the highway before Barby woke. Back in the house, he climbed the stairs cautiously. In the darkened bedroom, he fumbled for a suit, fresh linen. Arms laden, he crept past Barby's heavy breathing and dressed in the warm kitchen.

The fat white clock ticked loudly as he boiled water for tea, an egg. Someone had scribbled notes on the pad on the cupboard door. At the bottom of the list, the daily woman had written Kline's telephone number. Fraser wet a finger and carefully erased it.

It was almost nine. As he buzzed a day's beard from his face, he composed the note for Barby. Since yesterday, he had no doubt of her anxiety or its cause. The Patterson family took their doctors seriously. Solid men prescribing treatment and medicine for ailments rendered almost innocuous by their familiarity. Specialists drew the respect engendered by fame and success. That's about as far as it went. Psychosomatics—the esoteric language used by psychiatrists—would first startle then frighten the Pattersons. It was easy to imagine the broker's alarm at the mention of shock treatment. Their concern was less that Fraser was seeing a doctor than the wrong kind of doctor. After last night Barby would see that her father made no contact with the real Doctor Landers. What she did herself was a risk that had to be taken.

He wrote his message and left it propped against Barby's handbag. " Back as soon as I can, darling." It committed him to nothing beyond what it implied.

One eye on the curtained windows upstairs, he inched

the convertible past the dew-heavy grass. Mist was gathering on the windshield, running in dirty streaks. He set the wipers working. At the end of the driveway, he put the car into second gear and headed towards London.

At Tolworth, the roundabout-ridden highway was jammed with traffic. He pulled over to the side and called Kline's number from a vacant booth. The lawyer's voice was bland yet Fraser sensed the ready menace.

" Where are you speaking from ? " the lawyer asked quickly.

Fraser imagined the man's eye on the clock. He glanced at his watch. It was ten-thirty. It was good to hear the urgency in Kline's voice. Now the lawyer had troubles of his own, the blitz on nerves was no longer one-sided. " I got the message," he said. " I'll be there in a half-hour, with luck. Kline. . . ."

The lawyer's sucked breath interrupted him. " Be sure you are. It's important."

The glass-panelled booth was hot and stank of disinfectant. He wedged his toe in the door. " It's just possible that my wife has your number," he said carefully. " If she ever rings, tell her your place is one of Dr. Landers' consulting rooms. Just *one* of them," he emphasized.

" Dr. Landers' consulting rooms, madam," the lawyer intoned. " The doctor is waiting."

Fraser made fast time, using the car's power and the back doubles along the south bank of the river. He parked behind Harrod's and walked down through Hans Place. As he turned the corner, he recognized the grey Jaguar. Drummond had left his car in front of the Argentine Consulate-General. Fraser walked round to the front of

73

the automobile then to the rear. Fore and aft, small CD plates had been added.

A milkman was busy at the service entrance to Kline's block. Fraser climbed the concrete steps after him. When the man's wire basket clattered along the corridor, Fraser slipped through the pass-door. Kline answered the bell. He was wearing a double-breasted black jacket, striped trousers and a wide, winged collar. He both looked and smelt of high living. Chuckling, he led the way into the sunlit room. "Almost like old times," he said. "Remember those days, Kit?"

They weren't easily forgotten. Sequels to months of waiting, they recalled the dark silence of other people's houses. The weight of jewellery hefted in the hand—the money-littered table in Kline's house. The pay-off. They were neither forgotten. Nor regretted.

Drummond was lolling in an armchair, one leg thrown over the rest. His long straight hair was even blonder than Fraser remembered. In the grey overcheck suit and club tie, Drummond was indistinguishable at first sight from a thousand others of his class and age.

He stretched easily, a hand barely raised in greeting. His face was expressionless. "Kline's been telling me about the dog." Sun caught the glass of his wristwatch. He moved his arm idly, playing the light on the polished surface of the spinet. "What were you doing in South Street?" he asked suddenly.

Fraser took the seat opposite. Behind him, the bedroom door was open. Kline was moving about in there, humming. Fraser lined up the tips of his shoes, concentrating. "Looking," he said. "Why?"

Drummond's sprawl was superb. "I'll ask the questions. How old is the dog?"

Fraser pushed his shoulders deeper into the chair. " God knows. I saw it for maybe thirty seconds. At a guess, nine months."

Drummond nodded. He smiled, his voice friendly. " How did you deal with dogs in your day, Fraser ? "

" I avoided them," said Fraser.

" You mean because you're squeamish about such things ? " Drummond's eyes were curious.

" That's right," said Fraser steadily. " I was a Boy Scout too."

Drummond flicked his fingers over his shoulder. " It's a bloody nuisance," he said indifferently. Kline came to the bedroom door. " Give me the tools," said Drummond. He took the washleather bag juggling it from one hand to the other. " If you do have any ideas about the dog, I'd be glad to hear them. Before to-night if possible. I'll give it some thought myself meanwhile."

Fraser watched the bag—heard it chink as it landed in Drummond's palm. " A little thing like that won't bother you."

Drummond's eyes never left Fraser's face. " I've got a crippled bitch," he said flatly. " A drunk did it three years ago. I put him in hospital." He hitched his shoulders. " There's a difference between sentiment and sentimentality." He pulled himself out of his sprawl. " Have a look at these! "

Fraser's hand went out to catch the bag Drummond tossed at him. He opened it. Two of the keys inside were thin and functional—their operational parts reduced to a minimum. Skeleton keys of Vanadium steel as good as any he had ever seen. The third was shorter—its wards more complicated. It had a number stamped on its shank.

Kline was moving about like a stage butler, lowering the blinds on Fraser's side of the room. He leaned down, his breath unpleasantly close. " Organisation has improved since your day, my boy. Given the make and serial number of any safe—I can produce a duplicate in twenty-four hours." He screwed his face round and winked. " It's hardly legal but it's safe."

Fraser threw the bag back. Drummond trapped it neatly. " I've got a rim vice that takes care of the Ingersoll. It's ten minutes' work but it never failed yet." He passed the bag to Kline. " I've had these mortise keys a month. The dropped E was a bit long in the wards last time I fitted the place. It should be all right now. We'll see to-night."

Kline towered over his drink tray like a buzzard over a carcass. " Who wants a drink ? "

Drummond said no without bothering to turn his head. For some time now, his eyes had been on Fraser almost unblinkingly. Fraser took the glass Kline pushed into his hand. It was a weak mixture but welcome. He aimed his accusations at Kline but it was Drummond he looked at. " I've had it all this last forty-eight hours," he said bitterly. " Mysterious phone calls, fake cops. Enough crap to fill a dozen whodunits." Though his voice was on the rise nobody interrupted him. " You've pushed me where there's no place to go any more. All I know is that my liberty's at stake as well as your own." His hands were shaking. He grabbed the arm-rests. " All right," he shouted. " All right! "

" All right *what*, Kit ? " Kline said gently.

Drummond was on his feet, snarling at Kline. " Shut up, you fat oaf ! " He wrenched the shade back, letting sun to the room again. " Go and take a bath or something," he said contemptuously. He sat down again, smoothing the straight blond hair over his ears. He leaned forward, head propped in his hands. "What's worrying you, Fraser?"

In some subtle way, his well-being depended on equality with these people. He sought desperately for the right way in which to achieve it. "I've given you my word," he said hoarsely. "I'm committed. What I've done already's enough to finish me. Now I've got a right to know when it'll be over. When and how." Drummond made no answer. "About the dog . . ." Fraser started. "You say you've got to know by to-night. The keys . . ." he was still flustering for a formula that would preserve his conceit. First Barby now these bums. The fear must stink on him. "What *happens* tonight?" he asked quietly.

Kline started a throaty wheeze, one hand aloft as he prepared some pompous phrase. Drummond stopped him. "To-morrow night we're going into the Garrett house," he said evenly. Like a conjuror produces his surprise, Drummond held an engraved card in his hand. A five-guinea invitation for the following day.

Mrs. Chester Garrett will receive on behalf of the Anglo-American Society in the Banqueting Rooms of the Westminster Hotel, Park Lane.
8 p.m. *Dress Obligatory.*

Drummond put the card back in a crocodile wallet. "She doesn't know it," he smiled. "But she's going to receive me. I'm going to make sure she's at the Westminster then we'll go back to South Street and wait for her."

Kline stepped to Drummond's side, standing like a

fight manager behind some world champion. "Mark needs you to help him fit the door to-night, Kit. You know that's nothing," he soothed.

Fraser nodded. If the key did its job—turned off the lock—and you were caught at it, that was house-breaking. If they got you trying the key, the charge was attempted house-breaking. Even after eight years, the sweating terror of a key jammed in somebody else's lock was alive. He licked his mouth wet.

"You've got to be reasonable about this," he said half-heartedly. "My wife expects me back to-night." He caught fire remembering. "Ever since this thing started, you've been telling me to act normally at home. To-morrow's all right—I can fix that," he said doggedly. "But to-night's impossible."

Drummond lit a cigarette, watching the match flame die. His interest in Fraser seemed over. "What time does she expect you back?"

Fraser thought quickly. Keys were usually fitted at dead of night. When the house slept and you were free of alarm from the inside. He went through the moves in his mind. The turned lock—the slight push to make sure the door really opened. The click as it closed again. Then away. "Eight o'clock," he answered with what he hoped was assurance.

"Then that's no problem!" Drummond's smile was almost cheerful. "It's dark at six-thirty. You'll be home by eight."

Fraser carried his glass to the drinks-trolly. His back was to the younger man. He looked at Kline's smile sourly. "That sounds a crazy hour to fit a lock." Somehow he made his tone casual. "I suppose if you need me. . . ."

The room was suddenly quiet. A fly trapped between curtain and window buzzed, panic-stricken. " *Any* time I break the law in this venture, I'm going to need you," Drummond said softly. " Any time and all the time."

Fraser moved to the window. Across the way, children were playing in the square. Hung high in the air, a couple of men were cleaning the inside of a street lamp. He turned, with sudden distaste for the men he faced—for himself. " I'd forgotten what a lousy bunch thieves were," he said huskily. He shook his head. " You guys don't even trust one another! "

Drummond was resting his elbow on the side of the chair. He sighed at Fraser, using his cigarette as a gun barrel. " You use this word 'trust' overmuch," he observed. " Come to think of it, you're a little like Kline. You both tend to dramatics." He pitched the butt at the fireplace and stood in front of the mirror, adjusting his handkerchief. " This isn't a Scout Jamboree. I think I know human nature, Fraser. But I'm always ready to be agreeably surprised." He nodded at Fraser. " Meet me at six-thirty. Grosvenor Square, opposite the American Embassy." He grinned and his face showed real amusement. " The place is always thick with cops but where could there be a more respectable place to start or finish! "

Fraser suddenly remembered the CD plates. He followed Kline to the door. The lawyer kept one hand on the latch and used the other in a sort of benediction. " We're all in this far too deep to turn back, Kit. For anything. You understand, of course ? " It was more than a question.

Fraser sighed. As if for the hundredth time, he shook himself free from the other's touch. " What do *you* think ? " he answered and started down the stairs.

He made for the park, inevitably. It was a place to be free of people. He drove past the Palace and along the Mall, leaving the car by the Admiralty Arch. Once he had walked over the ornamental bridge, he turned deep into the shrubbery. A bench by the lake was empty. Duck drifted by on the dark-green water, waddled up the muddy slope to the thick reeds beyond. It was too late in the year for the office picnickers. He stretched himself out on the bench. Big Ben reared over the tops of the bowed willows. As familiar as an advertisement. East of it, just four or five hundred yards away, was New Scotland Yard. Somewhere in the Criminal Records Office a file had his name on it. Oddly enough that phoney cop had been right. They never forgot you at the Yard—no matter if a clutch of clergymen attested your good character. Even a Death Notice would be checked on before they shifted your file to the Inactive Section.

He moved uneasily, turning so that he stared straight up at the sky. The gulls flapped overhead in ever-widening circles. He couldn't get the dachshund out of his mind. That crack of Drummond's about squeamish-ness had been too apt. The guy had a trick of exposing the unpalatable—dredging up truths that you'd rather forget. Or ignore. If some animal bolted out on the high-way while you were driving, you swerved automatically—maybe with four people in the car. Chances were that the R.S.P.C.A. provided headstones. But what did you do in deliberation if a dog stood between you and achievement. Whether it was the theft of eighty-five thousand pounds' worth of jewellery or simply the end of blackmail.

Somehow, they had to deal with this dachshund. He went over the possibilites. Perhaps the chauffeur exer-cised the dog. He visualised the park—the uniformed man snatching a cigarette as the dachshund ran, barking. Drummond's elegant figure as he held the man's attention. Himself snatching the dog and hurrying it away. Easy to drive it to the Dogs' Home in Battersea—call the police or Mrs. Garrett once the refuge was closed. She'd know where her dog was but wouldn't be able to get it till next day. Or maybe she left the animal in her car while she was being gracious to the Anglo-American Society. There might be a chance to grab it then. The fancies lost conviction, one after another. These essays into dog-stealing were unprofitable. Let that old bag lose her pet and she would have a squad of cops on her doorstep till it was found. She had been burgled too many times.

The bench was hard. He sat up and looked at his watch. Lunch-time. Once he had eaten, a movie would be as good a place as any to kill the hours. He'd get to Grosvenor Square in good time. That way he would be sure of parking space. He started the long walk back to the car.

Dusk came disappointingly early. By six, lights already burned on the square. Three sides of the two hundred yards space were devoted to official representation of the United States Government. Sixty feet away, uniformed cops were patrolling the front of the Embassy. He cut his parking lights and sat watching them. Savile Row Police Station was only a half-mile away. By now the daytime thieves were back home—the night operators not yet out. There was possibly an hour before the plain-clothes men started slipping in pairs from the station-house. Men pulled off the beat, in civilian clothes, eager to make the grade to the detective branch. Only a little while before the local squad cars slid into the area. Most sinister of all, the fast black vehicles of the Flying Squad. Four or five men to a crew, the radio operator hidden behind bloomed

81

glass at the back of the car. He remembered the sudden
shock of coming upon a squad car waiting unexpectedly
round a corner. The desperation that forced you past the
waiting men. The expected hail. In an hour's time they'd
all be out. Routine patrol; playing a cop's hunch;
following some stool pigeon's tip.

He touched the dashboard light. It was six-twenty.
Traffic in the square was becoming sparser. The green
patch behind him was a sanctuary where all that lived was
still and safe for the night. The statue lost in the shadow
beyond the trees.

He started to empty his pockets methodically. Stowing
everything but cash, comb and keys in the locked glove
compartment. A card, a handkerchief, dropped in flight
and you woke in a cell instead of your own bed. In the
minutes that followed, he switched the radio first on then
off a dozen times. It was six twenty-five when a car came
fast from the direction of Grosvenor Street. Slowing for
the bend, the driver flashed his headlights a couple of
times. As the car passed, fifteen feet away, Fraser recognized the grey Jaguar.

Fraser climbed to the back of the big convertible.
Drummond had to make the sweep of the square before he
could park. The embassy guard across the way was
being relieved. For a moment the squad of police stood
chatting in the light of a street lamp. As the men moved
off, Fraser heard the tapping on the outside of the hood.
Drummond had walked round behind the line of parked
cars. Fraser opened the door. Drummond climbed into
the back with him.

There was enough light to distinguish Drummond's
face, his clothes. He was wearing the same suit as in the
morning—topped with a dark, fitted overcoat. An in-

congruous bowler shaded his eyes, tipped forward at the outlandish angle affected by the Brigade of Guards. He was carrying a large bunch of flowers wrapped in Cellophane bearing the name of a fashionable florist. Already the car was heady with the pungency of freesias. Drummond leaned back in the corner holding the flowers upright.

" How do you feel ? " he asked casually.

Drummond's trick of expecting to invest others with his private certainty irritated Fraser. He started pulling on his thin skin gloves.

Drummond wagged a finger. " Crêpe soles *and* gloves! Right out of page one of the Burglars' Handbook. And incidentally, the first thing a yokel with six months on the force looks for."

Fraser pulled his fingers away as though burned by the leather. He smoothed the thin hide nervously. The complete Gentleman-at-Crime, he thought. The man with all the answers. " Put them on later," Drummond said wearily. He pushed the flowers at Fraser. " Carry these. And keep them upright—the keys are hidden in the stems."

Fraser's fingers dug into the Cellophane till he felt metal through the stalks. For a second he thought of ramming the whole package into the other's face. *Anything* to stifle this series of lofty instructions. As if he sensed it, Drummond's mood changed. He was suddenly friendly. " You've got the sweats," he said gently. " It's the first job you ever did, all over again. Right ? "

" Worse," Fraser said with resentment. " I know too much now." Drummond gave the answer thought. He seemed tired. " I'd probably be uneasy if you didn't dislike me, Fraser. But we're in this together, like it or not. Just remember one thing. I do know what I'm doing!" He cupped hands round a match. Behind the twisting smoke his eyes were steady. "This isn't any boy-burglar's raid on the toffs—it'll be the biggest job of its kind in twenty years." He fanned himself with his hat then opened a window. "We've got a simple story if we're stopped," he said suddenly. "We're on our way to the Connaught for a drink. We parked here because there's always room." He gestured at the flowers. "And you're leaving those for Mrs. Garrett. Any questions?"

In spite of the fresh air, the interior of the car was still heavy with freesias. Drummond's calm educated voice invested the whole venture with unreality. Two men walking the streets of Mayfair carrying a bunch of flowers wrapped round skeleton keys! "I've never even met the woman socially," said Fraser. "What reason could there be for me giving her flowers?"

"Enough for anyone who might stop us," Drummond was amused, his sudden laugh loud. Fraser looked instinctively at the cops across the street. They stood at the base of the steps, immobile and indifferent. "You don't need a permit to give a woman flowers," said Drummond. He had one hand on the door catch. "Nobody's *going* to ask questions." He opened the door.

They crossed the square to Carlos Place. They walked shoulder to shoulder, without haste and with certainty. Drummond seemed to court the darkened doorways—the blind angles of street corners. A half-dozen times he raised his voice to relate some inane story. Holding the flowers carefully, Fraser managed an uneasy laugh.

Halfway down Mount Street, he felt Drummond's hand in warning on his sleeve. Without hesitation he went into an exaggerated American accent. A garbled monologue about furlough, stateside and the Colonel. Two men were standing in the shelter of an art dealers' doorway. He kept the story going as he passed them. His shoulders contracted as if to ward off their menace. Fifty yards on, Drummond's shoulder guided him into a mews. They walked its length then Drummond bent over his shoes, screwing his head round. The cobbled stretch was empty in the light from the hanging lamps.

As they entered South Street Drummond gave the instructions. " We'll go past the house. Then turn back and straight up the steps. Break the Cellophane and hand me the keys. You can cover me with the flowers."

Fraser nodded. Drummond's leather heels were making far too much noise. Fraser found himself tip-toeing in compensation. " If somebody opens the door . . ." he started.

" Give her the bloody flowers! " said Drummond savagely.

The Garrett house was lit on three storeys and in the basement. A bright lamp hung over the portico at the top of the steps. At the end of the street they stopped while Drummond scanned the house numbers osten-tatiously. " We've gone past," he said loudly.

Fraser touched his arm. " We can't go up those steps now," he whispered. " They've got a million lights on."

Drummond's shoulder shoved Fraser forward. " Start walking, you clod! " he said. His bowler hat was perched over his eyebrows. His mouth was thin. They walked up the steps. The iron railings gave no shelter. Curtains in the windows to the right were drawn. A car turned into the street. They waited till it had gone. At any minute Fraser expected a head to show in the window above them.

" Keys," whispered Drummond. Fraser broke the Cellophane with nervous fingers and pulled out the leather bag. Drummond leaned a gloved finger an inch above the bell-push. Very casually he glanced at his watch then moved closer to the door. Fraser shuffled forward. They stood, facing the house, as if awaiting an answer to their summons. A sudden noise from the basement turned their heads. The patch of light on the flagstones grew bigger. They watched as a woman slouched out, clumsy in carpet slippers. The cover of a garbage pail clanged then the door closed again. Fraser held the bouquet in front of his chest like a shield. Ready to thrust it into the arms of whoever came to the door and run. Masked by Fraser's body, Drummond's hands were busy with the locks. Heels were clicking up the other side of the street. Somehow Fraser managed to keep his head straight. Drummond bent deliberately as the footsteps drew abreast. He peered through the keyhole, shrugged then looked at his watch. It was perfect mime—the caller who recognizes that he is unwelcome. The two men turned and walked after the solitary pedestrian.

" They only had the Ingersoll on," said Drummond. He wiped the sweat from the band of his bowler. " Shove these back in the flowers," he said. " It isn't seven yet." His voice was pleased. " The keys are perfect. I turned both the mortises on and off. You'll be home by half-past eight."

Back in Grosvenor Square, they sat silent in the parked Buick. Fraser was unable to rid himself of a sudden sense of fellowship with the man beside him. A warmth that came from shared danger. His voice broke nervously. " The dog didn't make a sound. Maybe I was knocking myself out for nothing."

Drummond used Fraser's given name for the first time.

86

" Let me worry about the dog, Kit. You couldn't have done better to-night."

Fraser started filling his pockets with the things he'd left. Wallet, licence, keys. His mouth was still sour with fright, his shirtback damp.

Drummond's words put the whole crazy ordeal in perspective. Just one small accident and he'd be finished as surely as though Kline were to plaster his past over a two-page advertisement. Just one of the unforeseen hazards that beset a burglar. The lonely woman at a window, watching the street; the ankle twisted in flight; the small boy collecting licence tag numbers. Drummond's belief in himself drove past reason. Six years' endeavour tossed on the junk heap—Drummond's reaction—" You couldn't have done better to-night."

" What are you going to tell your wife about to-morrow night ? " asked Drummond.

Before, there'd never been any need to lie to Barby. They had lived, fought and made their peace with candour. During his restless times, he'd packed a bag and driven deep into the country. Barby neither asked nor did he explain where the trips took him. Christ knows, they were innocent enough. A second-rate boxing club in a Welsh mining town. A desolate beach where the sea sucked sand interminably. Once, perhaps in six months, this need was strong. For a few days he took off and lived among strangers. Unsharing and unshared. Then hurried home to a house warm with security. Content. Barby always understood—even hid his confusion from her parents.

" I'm not much good at lying to her," he answered. The next words came without reason. " Are you married ? "

Drummond's repose was complete. No nervous mannerisms betrayed his control. His breathing sounded relaxed and easy.

" Not yet," he said quietly. " I've never supposed I had the right." He shrugged, fishing for a cigarette. " Living this sort of life is complicated enough. Once this is over. . . ."

Ahead, the lighted hand on the clock neared the quarter hour. Something made Fraser go on. " I don't get it," he said awkwardly. He groped for a match, unsure of himself. " You and Kline. You don't even like him." he challenged suddenly.

Drummond took the light. " You don't *have* to get it." He leaned back, the cigarette end red in the darkness. " You happened to be lucky. You found your alternative to thieving. I've had to wait till I could buy mine. All my life I've been doing things I disliked." His laugh was self-mockery. " I'm worried about your wife. Suppose I phoned you at ten in the morning. Who'd answer ? "

Fraser shrugged. " It depends. It could be me."

" Suppose you don't take the call ? You know it'll be me and don't answer ? "

" Then Barby'd probably take it—my wife. Or the woman."

Drummond sounded satisfied. " Then to-morrow I'll phone as your doctor. You've got to spend a night at the clinic."

Fraser lowered the window suddenly. He peered out at the car that had been parked at the end of Carlos Place for the past ten minutes.

" Just a man talking to a woman," Drummond said easily. " Possibly a whore. How does that story sound to you, Kit ? "

" It isn't me you have to convince," Fraser pointed out.
" My wife's likely to be less suspicious of the story than the
doctor. She mistrusts all mental specialists."

Drummond's hands were behind his neck—the hat
tipped completely over his eyes. " I see. You know—I
could almost sleep in the back of this thing." He was
silent for a moment.

" Don't worry! " he said suddenly. " I'll make
Landers sound as respectable as the Queen's Physician."
His voice took on a testy Scots accent. " It's *Mrs.* Fraser
I'm talking to! Aye—I doubt you'll have been anxious,
Mrs. Fraser. But your husband has responded to the
treatment pairfectly. Pairfectly! A wee while and you'll
have him back as guid as new." He yawned. " Come to
think of it, that's literally true. Do you know any of the
jargon these fellows use ? " he asked.

" I've been reading it," admitted Fraser. All that
mattered was keeping Barby convinced till this was over.
He looked at the clock. " O.K. What time to-morrow
and where ? " he asked steadily.

" Kline's at seven. We can have a quick bite there and
get about our business." Drummond's voice was friendly.
" Don't think about it too much. I can see from to-night
you're going to be all right."

" I *know* I'll be all right," lied Fraser. " You must have
some idea what all this means to me, Drummond," he
he said impulsively. " I don't trust Kline an inch. But
you've given me your word. . . ."

Drummond sat up. " This will probably shatter your
tribal loyalties still more—*I* don't trust Kline. But you can
rest assured of this. When I said you'd hear nothing more
from either of us—once this is over—I meant it."

Fraser nodded secret belief. " Seven," he promised.

"Wear dark clothes," said Drummond. "And to-morrow night you'll certainly need gloves."

"I'm not likely to forget," said Fraser. "Here—you'd better take these." He pushed the bunch of flowers across the seat.

Drummond set the bowler carefully on his head. "Give them to your wife," he said indifferently. He shut the car door and walked off into the dark square.

When he no longer heard the sound of footsteps, Fraser dropped the Cellophaned package through the window. Beyond Guildford, the road was both dry and deserted. He made fast time to Two Bridges.

He braked suddenly at the end of the driveway to his home. Lights burned upstairs and downstairs. He peered out. Shadows moved behind the guest-room curtains. He drove the Buick round to the yard. His father-in-law's car stood in the garage. Fraser felt the top of the radiator. It was barely warm. Patterson must have been here some time.

He cut the lights and stood in the garage, watching the house. The last time his father-in-law had arrived un-announced had been four years ago. At three in the morning with the roads all but impassable after a January blizzard. Upstairs, the village doctor had eased Barby through the shock of a premature and stillborn child. It took no less to jolt Patterson from a routine as unvarying as that of a church almanack.

He put his car into the second stall and pulled down the door. He couldn't forget the piece of paper he'd given Kline. Suppose the policy details had come into the hands of the police. He scotched the thought with an effort and crossed the yard. Whatever the reason for Patterson's visit, it had to be faced.

The light came on inside as he opened the kitchen door. Barby was standing there, hair tawny above the pale-green woollen dress. She was wearing fur-topped boots.

" Hello, darling! " Her head was down as she fished in the icebox for lager. It was impossible for him to see her expression. " Daddy's here," she said.

Fraser looked at her guardedly. She'd said nothing about him being late.

She put the beer on a tray and shook her hair back. " I said Daddy's here, darling," she repeated.

" I heard you," he said shortly and slumped in a chair to fumble with his slippers.

She knelt, easing his feet into shabby leather with her hands. " There," she said gently. " The meal's waiting. All you two men have to do is eat it." She opened the door to the hall. At the sound of his voice she came back to the kitchen carrying a Burberry. He closed the door and stood with his shoulders against it.

" What is all this in aid of ? " he asked heavily.

" You've got that pulse in your forehead again, Kit! " she warned. She touched his skin lightly.

He took hold of her wrist. " I'm going over to Kate Gilmour's for an hour." She spoke so quietly that he barely heard her. " Jim's not back."

" The hell with Jim! " he burst out. " I asked you what all this was in aid of ! " He jerked his head at the closed door behind him. " What's your father doing here ? "

She dragged her wrist free. " You're hurting me," she complained. He touched the thin skin at his temple. " What's he here for ? " he repeated.

She put the beer and glasses on a tray, avoiding his look. " Let me by, Kit. Come on—I've got to take these in! "

91

He made no move to let her pass. " I get it –the man-to-man talk with you conveniently out of the way," he said staring at her. " You're going to tell me *why*! "

She put the tray back on the table and braced herself. " Don't you *know* why ? " she asked.

" Hell! " he said bitterly. " Is it any wonder I've finished in a psychiatrist office! Living in a house crawling with mystery! "

He scuffed after her into the living room, slipper heels flapping.

Patterson climbed up from his chair. He was flushed from the fire and comfortable in grey tweeds. " Hello, Kit! I suppose Barby's told you you've got to put up with me for the night. Her mother's down at Arborfield."

Fraser nodded. " We're very glad to have you, sir." Patterson's face was innocent of all accusation.

Barby hovered as the two men sat at the table. Heaping plates of food, pouring each glass of beer with care. " All right, you two," she said finally. " And you're not to worry about washing up the stuff. Just dump the things in the sink. Mrs. Ellis will take care of them in the morning."

Her father shook his head affectionately. " You're not going out in this cold without eating yourself ! "

" Kate'll boil us an egg or something," she said easily. She kissed each in turn and was gone.

The two men ate quickly, skirting holes in the conversational ice. Finished, Fraser carried the trays to the kitchen. When he came back, Patterson had stretched his long legs to the fire. He had a pipe going, a glass of brandy cupped in his hands.

Fraser dimmed the lights and took the other armchair. " Now, sir," he said determinedly.

Patterson blinked, manœuvring his pipe. "It's no good being angry with Barby," he said mildly. "A woman's loyalty to her husband runs peculiar courses. You mustn't resent it, Kit. Barby's confided in me because she loves you." He got up from his chair to settle his back against the mantel. The office position, thought Fraser. The old boy felt happier like that. He warmed to Patterson suddenly, the urge strong to confide in his father-in-law. He knew that within the rigid framework of his character, Patterson loved him. He watched the thin gentle face with compassion. It was no use —he had to work this thing out alone—free of the curbs that confession entailed. Only one thing mattered. An end to the evil that threatened them all. He must finish it single-handed as best he may.

This was no longer a tale of a criminal record hidden over the years. But a confession of confidential information passed on to thieves—of a personal commitment to robbery. Once Patterson knew the truth, he could do but one thing—face Lloyd's Committee with a six-year list of burglary policies affected by a convicted thief. Then close his business.

No matter how far the Committee at Lloyd's would lean for the sake of an honoured firm, there *was* no alternative. He pictured the sordid sequence. Cops with long memories, suspicious of motive. A criminal trial during which Kline extracted each damaging truth till he was able to drag everyone down in his personal disgrace.

Patterson put his brandy glass on the shelf behind him. He lifted his coat tails, grunting pleasure as the warmth reached his buttocks.

"I don't have to tell you how close Barby and I have been," he said. "Ever since she was old enough to *have*

93

troubles, she brought them to me rather than to her mother. That's really why she's come to me now! "

" Yes, but came to you with *what*, sir ? " The facets of the cut-glass tumbler made good fingerholds. He dug in.

" Very little really," Patterson assured him. " And I want to impress on you that her mother knows nothing. Absolutely nothing! "

Fraser lifted the tumbler to his mouth, two-handed. Then he spoke very deliberately. " We're talking at cross-purposes, sir. Unless you tell me what Barby has said to you, I can only guess."

The older man moved back to his chair. " Well," he said. " About this doctor, for example. She's worried about him. I can't say I blame her." He looked over the top of his glass. " Most of these so-called mental specialists are quacks." Fraser said nothing. " I've sensed something wrong these past few weeks," said Patterson. " I wasn't in the least surprised when Barby told me you were "—he shrugged "—feeling under the weather."

At any other time, it would have been laughable. This kindly old man so wise after the event. And so completely wrong.

Patterson stretched his legs to the fire again. He glanced at the door before lowering his voice. " I always look on you and Barby as an ideal couple. The fact that she's my daughter is incidental." He turned so that he faced Fraser, his thin hand clenched till it was bloodless. " Difficulties are *part* of our relationship with women, Kit. I'm going to be absolutely frank with you—it'll make me happy if you confide in me. There's no question of anything like blackmail, is there ? "

Shock froze the tumbler half-way to his mouth. He set it down on a carpet a thousand miles away. His voice seemed to echo in a tunnel. " What makes you say a thing like that ? " he whispered.

" You say you have no money worries. There's a bright future in front of you," said Patterson. " And you have Barby. Suddenly you go to pieces. So much so that Barby's worried sick over it. There isn't some other woman, is there ? " the old man asked gently.

" No," said Fraser. " No, there isn't. Barby's the only one I've ever loved."

" That doesn't answer my question," Patterson said quietly. " Kit—nobody knows better than I how easy it is for a chap to get into a mess over a woman."

" I said there's no other woman and no blackmail, sir." For a moment, the two men looked at one another in silence. " I'll give you my word on that," said Fraser suddenly.

" That's enough for me." Patterson sat up and sipped his drink. " You don't know how relieved I am to hear you say that, Kit. Some day I'd like to tell you a story . . ." he let his breath go in a deep sign. " That leaves just one thing—this doctor of yours."

Fraser made another trip to the decanter. Not even here at home could he relax for one second. The feeling of isolation was intolerable. " What about him ? " he asked from behind Patterson's back. As he poured, he sensed his father-in-law compose himself for diplomacy.

" I happened to be having a word with Doctor Murdoch," Patterson said carefully. " Of course you'll think of him as an old fogey but he's sound." He wriggled his shoulders. " All these mental fellows are just groping, you know, Kit. There's very little we know about the working of the human mind, in reality." He nodded a couple of times. " Thank God! " he said fervently.

95

Fraser crossed in front to kick the logs. It wasn't hard to imagine Patterson's G.P. Some snuff-nosed old Scot, sure and skilled in the tradition of the '20's. He propped a heel on the fire-surround and stared at his father-in-law sombrely.

Patterson sounded embarrassed. " If I'm taking too much on myself, Kit, say so! Personally I doubt if there's much wrong with you that a rest won't cure." The smile made Patterson's face young. " I don't intend to be one of these chaps who works so long that work becomes his only pleasure. That's why I'm going to need you, Kit. Strong and healthy."

Two days, he thought. In two days' time it would be over. In a few more days, he would be back at the office. For the first time the realisation hit him. From now on, every mark of confidence his father-in-law showed—every kindness—would be a reminder of treachery.

" I shouldn't worry about this doctor," he urged. " It's possible that everything you say is true. But the man is helping me." His voice was loud and his whole body shook. " You've got to believe me," he burst out. " I need this treatment—the worst way. Barby should know! " He threw a hand at the warm pink room. " She's had to live with me these past few days. But it's done with," he said vehemently. Sweat covered his neck and he moved from the fire. " A couple of days and I'll be all right," he mumbled.

" I'm sure you will," soothed Patterson. " The fact that you believe in this fellow is half the battle."

They sat in companionship till the scrape of the back door signalled Barby's arrival. She came in ruddy-cheeked with cold, the fur around her ankles spiked with moisture. She went over to the fire to hold out her hands,

shivering dramatically. " I'm not sure it won't freeze
to-night. What does the forecast say ? "

Fraser answered. " We didn't listen," he said shortly.

" You're both ready for bed," she announced. " Come
on—bed for everyone." She covered her father's eyes
with her fingers, looking askance at Fraser. He nodded.
" Daddy, I want no nonsense from you! " She rubbed her
cheek against her father's. " You've got an electric
blanket. And you're to keep it on."

Patterson pulled himself up, grumbling. " Good-night,
Kit," he gave his hand to Fraser. " Good-night, my boy,"
Patterson repeated. In the flickering firelight he looked
old. Old and helpless.

By the time he had finished in the bathroom, Barby was
in bed. Shiny-faced in a highnecked nightgown she
looked like a child. He sat on the edge of his own bed.
There were things he wanted to say but the lie he was
living robbed him of confidence. He touched the light
button and opened the window.

The moon rose on its back beyond the hills. Past the
silver-green grass the firs were black and silent. The sound
of a barking dog came clear in the still air. He climbed
into bed and lay there staring at the ceiling. The bed-
clothes rustled as she turned towards him.

" Do you hate me sometimes ? " she asked. He was too
near breaking point to answer. " I could understand it if
you did," she went on in a small voice. " I just won't give
up worrying about you—for you."

He wrenched himself up on an elbow. " I could never
hate you," he said with truth. " I think since I've known
you, about everything I've done consciously has been . . ."
He struggled for words. " God, Barby, I *love* you! "

" Kit, darling! " Her voice was muffled as she wriggled

97

deeper under the covers. Suddenly she giggled. " I can imagine what Daddy said. Man-to-man stuff about was there another woman! "

He lowered his head to the pillow, still watching her. " Right."

" And was there ? "

" Three," he said solemnly.

Her laugh was happy. " I could have told Daddy better. Poor Daddy! It's not fair, Kit." She was serious again. " I know you love me. Yet after all these years I sometimes wonder whether you know me. That's far more difficult."

" Like a bad penny," he told her.

" I'm not so sure," she said quietly. She pounced on his silence. " Would you come to me if you were in real trouble ? You *could*, Kit. I'd destroy anything that threatened your happiness. Or anyone."

Memory blazed. But he made his words kind. " You wanted to leave me once—when I first met you. I wasn't even *in* any kind of trouble then."

She made a small contemptuous sound. " That was different and you know it! You had that ridiculous chip on your shoulder. Wanting everybody to know how wicked you had been. Just like a small boy wanting to shock people. Another thing. . . ."

Moonlight touched the end of her bed. He saw that she was smiling. " What ? " he asked.

" I'm not so sure that I wasn't just infatuated with you then," she answered. " It's different now. I have to go as you go, Kit. You see, you're my life."

He kicked the covers of his bed free, then crossed the room and sat on the edge of her bed. For a moment he held her face in his hands. As he bent his head he felt the warm comfort of her arms around him. He pushed his head against her breasts, lost and afraid.

He awoke easily and with a sense of impending excitement. Barby was still sleeping beside him, huddled under the covers. Her hair had spread on the pillow like a chestnut fan. It was a quarter-to-eight. The tray with the tea-things was by the bed. He plugged in the kettle and stood by the window.

A haze hung low above the trees, screening the early sun. The lawn was lacy with hoar frost—littered with oak leaves freed by the cold night. He shut the window quietly. Barby hadn't stirred in her bed. He was on his way to the bathroom when he heard Patterson's rasping cough—his guarded call. He stood outside his father-in-law's bedroom then tapped on the door and went in.

Patterson's hair stood incongruously on end—his cheeks sunken without his teeth. He stretched, yawned and looked at the window. " Good morning, Kit! It's almost worth enduring the rain to get a morning like this. Is Barby up ? "

Fraser grinned. " She will be when that kettle boils! " He moved about uncertainly to stand by the dressing-table. Patterson's belongings were ranged in neat order—the change in piles according to value. There was a small leather frame with a picture of Barby, schoolgirl vintage. The frame was worn, the child solemn.

" I never got the chance last night, sir," Fraser said hesitantly. " But I would like you to know that I'll be doing my best in the future." He tried to package his meaning in words that would register. " I'll make up for everything."

Patterson creaked out of bed—tried a couple of tottering knee-bends. He straightened up to smile ruefully.

99

"There's nothing to make up for, my boy." He started as something downstairs hit the front door with a thud.

"The newspapers," said Fraser.

Patterson wrapped himself in a tartan robe. He was happier with his teeth. "It takes crises for people to really get to know one another," he said.

"You won't mind if I use the bathroom first?" Patterson said. "*Somebody* had better represent the family at the office."

"You go right ahead," Fraser answered. He knew with certainty now that for Patterson he was no longer the stranger who had married Barby—but the son the old man had always wanted. He brushed through the door, resenting the shame he felt.

The three of them ate breakfast in the sun room. Barby was full of the next week's steeplechasing—caustic over the sports writers' sweeping prophecies. Patterson munched toast stolidly, shielding his eyes from the sun with *The Times*.

Outside in the garden, the haze had gone. The red-brick walks steamed in the sun. The fat dahlias were a blaze of colour along the east wall. Pretty soon, he thought, the man would be lifting the tubers. They'd hang over the garage, wrapped in burlap. With the stored apples, the saws, the axe. Up in the cool dry loft where he cleaned and oiled his guns at the end of a day in the woods beyond. These were good memories—a promise somehow that those things would continue.

Patterson lowered his newspaper. "One of our clients is in the news again, Kit. One of *your* clients, I should say!"

It took little now to trip the hammer in his chest. But he knew this answer before he asked the question. He kept his voice casual. " That right ? Who, this time ? "

" Mrs. Chester Garrett." Patterson's dry old mouth drooped uncompromisingly.

Fraser buttered an unwanted piece of toast very carefully. " And what's she doing ? "

Barby put her paper down. She was wearing jodhpurs —a sweater the colour of fudge. " Hey, that's the woman with the fabulous diamonds." She stretched out a hand. " Show me, Daddy," she demanded. She spread the paper across the table and pored over it.

Patterson rapped a thin finger on the newspaper. " If you women knew the trouble that these fabulous diamonds cause her," he said judiciously, " you wouldn't be so envious! "

" I'm not in the least bit envious," answered Barby. She clenched a small brown fist, holding it so that the sun struck light from the aquamarine. " I wouldn't swop this for *all* her jewellery. What's she like, Kit ? " she asked curiously.

" Aye, what *is* she like ? " Patterson repeated. " You know I never met her! "

To-morrow this conversation might be remembered. He had to leave an impression of normal interest—no more. " She's hard," he said after a moment's consideration. " That's the first thing that strikes you. Dead sure of her own importance to the world. And very rich. That about covers it. What's she doing ? " he asked again.

" Sponsoring some reception or something." Barby emptied her coffee-cup and folded the paper roughly. " She sounds a bore."

It was almost ten when Patterson turned the Rover on to the gravel. Fraser stood with Barby till the car was lost in the trees.

101

The windows were open in the living-room. As the phone rang stridently, he went down on one knee poking a stick at a daisy root. Barby stood by the bird platform tightening a wire. " Phone, Kit," she called.

He held up his hands covered in soil. " Will you get it ? "

As soon as she had gone inside, he bent double under the window. It was too far for him to distinguish her words. When she came out he was back at his digging.

" Kit! " He looked up. She brushed some dirt from his sweater nervously. " That was Doctor Landers."

He dumped the weeds on the gravel. " What's he want ? "

She held the soft wool tight. " You've to go to the clinic this afternoon—and spend the night there, he says." Her face was puzzled. " What on earth for ? "

He held his dirty hands high and solemnly kissed the end of her nose. " I thought we'd finished all that! " he warned. " Wait till I get my hands washed."

She followed him into the house—to the bathroom. Holding a towel while he scrubbed his nails clean. " What did he say exactly ? " he asked.

She looked bewildered. " Something about an injection sodium—soda—can't remember. But why at night ? "

He threw the soiled towel in the basket. " Sodium Pentathol," he said knowledgeably. " He said something about it the other day. It's a shot they give you at the end of the treatment. You do a lot of talking under the influence. Kind of clears out your subconscious. You want to throw a few things in a bag, darling ? " he asked quietly. " A toothbrush—pyjamas."

He went upstairs and took off his slacks and sweater. He chose a navy-blue suit, black shoes and tie, a dark overcoat. When he was dressed he called to her. " I think I'll go up before lunch, Barby."

She stood, the overnight bag in her hand. " Why? The man said this afternoon." She was looking at his suit, his tie. " You look so strange in those clothes." Her mouth worked. " Dressed for a funeral." Dropping the bag, she ran to him—hid her face on his shoulder. He held her close. " Stop it! " he stroked her hair gently.

She looked up wet-eyed. " I'm coming up with you," she said determinedly. " I can come to the clinic with you and spend the night with Mummy and Daddy."

He wiped the corners of her eyes. " Don't be foolish, darling. It's nothing more than a jab with a needle and a lot of chatter. God! " he grinned. " I don't want you eavesdropping on all my secrets! "

She worried him like a terrier, shaking the lapels of his jacket. " Promise you'll phone! "

" Sure, I'll phone," he said. " You know, this means the end of the treatment, Barby. Landers is sure I'll be back to normal in a couple of days. Look, I'll phone about eight. They'll probably have me in bed early—O.K ? "

She nodded, woebegone. " Even if it's only for a second but phone! "

He took the driveway slowly, seeing the frosted firs as if for the first time. Splayed tracks in the white rime marked where the crows had been. Broad arrows, he thought with distaste.

In London, he drove into a Park Lane garage that stayed open the clock round. Every move he made now was planned and self-protective. He emptied his pockets. Stuffing papers, keys and licence into the glove compartment, locking it. He gave the attendant a story of some party that might last all night and found a cab. His car was no more than a couple of hundred yards from the Garrett house. And off the street.

He dropped the cab at Canada House and climbed the broad steps. In the old days, he'd been used to ducking in and out of the place in a hurry—sweating the fifty yards from entrance to Mail Desk. The High Commissioner's office viewed his notoriety with disapproval. There'd been talk of withdrawing his passport—leaving him with a permit that would allow him to land in Canada and no more.

He found a corner in the Reading Room and sat down to write a couple of letters. One to Barby, the other to Patterson. He put both letters in a large envelope, addressing it to himself at Two Bridges. He dropped the package in the mailbox with a sense of finality. If he wasn't there to open it himself, the contents would be self-explanatory. With morbid interest, he killed the rest of the day in the Central Criminal Courts.

By the time he reached Pont Street, the lights were on. A few pedestrians hurried by, muffled against the raw air. Overhead, stars glittered in a clear night sky. The moon was fat. He walked down the concrete slope to the side entrance. The doors did not move. Through the glass he saw the bar was up inside. He made his way to the front of the block. The lobby was warm, sharp with the scent of the mink-coated women who waited for their cars. He reached the elevator unchallenged. He kept his head bent, showing as little as possible of his face to the operator. He got off at the floor above Kline's. As soon as he heard the whine of the falling cage, he started down the steps to Kline's apartment. Perhaps it was a useless stratagem. Yet the nearer the coup, the safer he felt leaving no gratuitous memories of his visits here.

The lawyer opened the door. Both he and Drummond were wearing dinner jackets. The room itself wore a festive air. Over on the spinet, an enormous spray of jasmine flanked the picture of Kline's wife. Ice piled about the bottle in the wine cooler. The table silver was bright. Throughout the room, the rich atmosphere of Kline's oriental cigarettes persisted.

Drummond smiled welcome. Dressed as he was in black, his hair had the colour of new straw. He cocked his head, considering Fraser's choice of clothes. Then he nodded approval. " Perfect! " he said. " This bloody moon's a nuisance, but with luck we shouldn't be long getting in."

Kline bent over the table ponderously. Surprisingly deft-handed, he moved a fork—a napkin. He took a step back to admire his work. " Now," he intoned. " Food! " He looked from one to the other. " You've no idea what a difference this deep-freeze stuff has made to my housekeeping. Simplified my problems beyond measure."

From behind Kline's back, Drummond winked at Fraser. " You're pompous enough for a bishop, Kline. But you haven't got the legs."

Fraser forced himself through the meal somehow. The other two ate with interest. They might have been catching a snack before leaving for the theatre. He twisted his long-stemmed glass nervously. He needed another drink and hadn't the courage to ask for one.

" Empty your pockets! " Drummond said suddenly.

Kline padded out to the hall—reappeared walking with Fraser's topcoat as if he were testing rotten floorboards. He explored each pocket. " Nothing! " It was difficult to tell whether he was pleased or not.

Drummond propped his elbows on the table. He

leaned his face in his hands, watching. The pile in front of Fraser grew. The stub from the garage. A few pounds in bills and change. A couple of handkerchiefs. An envelope.

Drummond reached across and took stub and envelope. " There's not much point leaving your identification in your car and carrying these." He threw the stub on one side. He looked at a snapshot of Barby thoughtfully, then returned it to its envelope. " Leave these here," he said quietly. " They're too easily dropped." He nodded at Kline.

" Stand up, Kit! " The lawyer faced Fraser. " Take off your shoes." Kline bent over, breathing heavily, rapping each shoe on the carpet. Certain that nothing was concealed, he gave the shoes back to Fraser. Then, like a prison searcher, he covered every inch of Fraser's body—the lining of his collar, his tie. He lifted his heavy shoulders. " He's got nothing, Mark."

Poker-faced, Drummond started to empty his own pockets. When he was done, he got to his feet and faced Fraser. He held his arms wide. " Go ahead," he invited. He straddled as Fraser patted his thighs, felt in the lining of his jacket.

Drummond retied his shoe-laces. The three sat at the table. Drummond tossed a set of car keys across to Fraser. " I've got a Sunbeam saloon downstairs. It's inconspicuous and fast enough for anything we might need. You're going to drive." He straightened his bow-tie. " Don't worry about being in a stolen car. I had a lot of fun in the car park. Putting the Sunbeam plates on a Ford. The Ford's on something else. I switched five sets altogether." He smiled, taken by the fancy. " The plates on the car now are from a wreck, in the breakers' yard."

He pushed his chair back and walked to the window. " Is there anything you want to get straight before we move, Kit ? "

These last few minutes Fraser had completely lost the fear of failure in the robbery. He just wanted it to be over. " I'd like a general idea of our plan," he said slowly. " And somewhere along the line I've got to find time to call my wife. About eight I said I'd call." Kline listened sleepy-eyed as the other two talked. " She thinks I'm at the clinic," Fraser reminded.

" Call her from the Westminster," said Drummond carelessly. " That's where we go from here. How did it go this morning ? " he asked with sudden curiosity. " How did your wife take it ? "

" She wasn't any too happy," Fraser answered. He pocketed the car keys, thinking. A Sunbeam had four forward speeds. This would be no time to foul up a gear shift.

Cigarette smoke drifted in front of Kline's face. He leaned forward, brushing it aside impatiently. " There wouldn't be any chance of her doing something stupid, would there ? "

" Such as what ? " Fraser asked.

Drummond's tanned face was expressionless. " What would *you* expect her to do, Kline ? "

The lawyer hitched his chair closer. " You know what women are. If she took it into her head to phone this Doctor Landers ——" his hand came up like a witness taking an oath. " I say '*if*' Mark," he emphasized. " What number would she call, Kit ? "

Fraser knew Drummond was watching him intently. He remembered the telephone number so carefully erased from the kitchen block. Pictured Barby searching the phone book—telephoning the genuine clinic. "She isn't going to call anybody." He drained his empty glass. "But if she did, she'd call here, I suppose."

The answer had stilled the wariness in Drummond's eyes. He nodded. "He knows his own wife, Kline. You're going to be here all night. If Mrs. Fraser does call, remember to give her the answer she wants."

"A thought, dear boy. No more than a thought," hurried the lawyer. He smiled apology at the two men.

"We're past the thinking stage," Drummond said dryly. "Listen, carefully, Kit. We park in the forecourt of the Westminster if there's room. If not, as near to the hotel as possible. You'll have to wait long enough for me to get into the Banqueting Room, no more. Once I've seen Mrs. Garrett, I know she's good for two or three hours at least. Then we'll drive to South Street, leaving the car at the side of the R.N.V.R. Club. Know it?"

Fraser nodded assent. The club angled the corner of Hill and Waverton Streets. Anyone in a car parked at the side of it could control the street door of the Garrett house. He walked over to the drinks-trolly and mixed himself a weak brandy and soda.

"The street door isn't going to be easy, is it?" He advanced his reason cautiously. "There's moonlight."

The other two men looked at one another. Kline rumbled the beginning of a reply but Drummond beat him to it. He swivelled his chair to face Fraser. "It isn't the moon as much as the dog that complicates things. We're not going in by the front door!" He was watching Fraser's reaction. "We're going to use the top back windows—the servants' bedrooms. The dog'll be downstairs with any luck till she gets back." He shrugged. "If not we'll have to deal with it."

" Deal with it," Fraser echoed the words like a talis-man. He carried his glass to his seat carefully. " How do we reach the windows ? "

" Get the gear," Drummond said to Kline. The lawyer came from the bedroom carrying a fibre-glass suitcase. He lifted it on to the table.

Drummond flipped the catches open. Inside was a tubular metal ladder telescoped to show a couple of rungs. Packed between the struts, skin-diving goggles, a pair of small black pistols. Drummond weighed one in his palm. " German alarm pistols," he said softly. " You know about these, Kit ? " Fraser shook his head. They looked like small Brownings. Yet there was a difference. A yellow cartridge was screwed into each barrel. " Tear-gas," said Drummond.

Fraser touched the barrel to his nose. It smelt faintly of peardrops. Drummond dangled the goggles from a finger. " We've got to wear these whether we use the pistols or not." He pushed one over the table. " Try it."

Fraser pulled the thing over his eyes. The two men faced one another, eyes hidden behind the amber mica. Drummond was grotesque with his straw hair and elegant dinner jacket. Fraser tore off the mask with relief.

Drummond had the ladder on the table. He pulled its length till a catch clicked. It was now twice as long. Again and again he did it till the extended ladder reached across the room from door to window. " My birds-nester's special! " Drummond touched the dull alumin-ium appreciatively. " This thing'll support five hundred pounds extended to twenty feet," he assured Fraser. " Made to my specifications in Belgium. For robbing eagles' nests," he grinned.

109

Kline wagged his head at Fraser, cracking his knuckles. " I told you Mark knows what he's doing."

Fraser ignored him. " The windows are belled," he said slowly. " Didn't you read that paper I gave Kline ? "

Drummond tried the weight of the closed case. " I did. The top windows aren't belled. We'll go in through the churchyard." He checked his watch, completely relaxed.

Kline lit another cigarette, his eyes bright. " There's no change as far as I'm concerned, Mark ? "

" No, you stay here till Fraser comes back with the swag." Drummond turned to Fraser. " Once we're out of the house, you'll drive my car here while I get rid of the Sunbeam." He stood in front of the mirror. He patted his hair flat, tugged the ends of his bow. " Are you ready, Kit ? "

Kline carried the case to the door. Big and benign, he shook hands with each in turn. " Good luck, Mark! Kit, there's a bed for you here later." He smiled. " I won't be likely to go to sleep till you're back." He handed the case to Drummond. " Go out by the side door. Leave the bar up. None of the night staff moves from the lobby after midnight. I'll go down later and make sure the door's still open." He peeped into the corridor then waved them out. The door closed quietly.

They hurried down the stone steps to the service exit. Drummond lifted the bar, pulled the doors shut after them. It was cold outside after the steam-heated flat. The concrete slope down to the garages glittered in the moonlight. A black saloon stood in front of the lock-ups.

" That's it," said Drummond.

Fraser unlocked the Sunbeam. Easing himself behind the wheel, he adjusted the driving seat. A second bag was already in the back of the car. Drummond propped the fibre-glass case between front and rear seats. As Fraser put the key in the ignition lock, Drummond caught him by the wrist. " Hold it! " He tucked one leg under the other, hitching his body nearer Fraser. His tone had none of its usual irony—he sounded strangely diffident. " There's something I've got to say before we go. I've told you you'll never hear of me after to-morrow. Have you understood that I mean it ? "

Fraser lit a cigarette. In this one thing, he had always believed Drummond. In spite of that first quick hatred, he accepted the man's word. " I've had no choice," quietly. " But I believe you."

" Good." Drummond sounded pleased. " I can be sure of myself but not Kline —do you understand that as well ? "

Fraser had the same sense of shock as though a friend had betrayed him. " I see. All this is probably for nothing as far as I'm concerned. For all you know I can have Kline on my back for the rest of my life. Is that it ? " He laughed shortly. " You've chosen a great time to tell me."

" That *isn't* it! " said Drummond.

It was light enough to see pedestrians on the sidewalk, thirty yards away. Fraser crushed out his cigarette. He looked at Drummond's impassive face, his steady eyes. " Then what ? "

The old humourless smile was back. " I put that wire recording in the post with the set, this afternoon. You should get it at Two Bridges to-morrow. When Kline's done his share in all this, we'll let him know." He sat up in his seat. " You'll have no trouble with him once he knows you've got that recording," he promised. He pointed at the ignition key. " Start her up! I've had everything checked. Oil, petrol, water and lights."

111

Fraser touched the button. The motor idled without a tremor. Drummond reached behind, hand on the raw-hide case. " There's a change of shoes and clothing here for both of us. Once we leave the Garrett house, we get rid of every stitch we're wearing now. I don't intend to leave the slightest chance for the boys at the Forensic Lab. to get busy with their chemistry sets."

Fraser put the car up the slope. Wheels spun, then caught, sending the Sunbeam surging out to the street. Drummond grabbed the handbrake, stalling the motor. " Take it easy," he said quietly. " Keep a normal speed all the time. We want no trouble with traffic cops."

At the Sloane Street signals, Fraser took his place in the northbound traffic. He was using the exaggerated caution of a man fresh from driving school. Drummond lolled, body half-turned so that he could watch the back window unostentatiously. They drove into the park and out at Stanhope Gate. Park Lane was thick with the theatre rush. A white-sleeved pointsman held the east-bound stream. Fraser took a look at the forecourt of the Westminster. Cars packed the space in front of the fountain.

" Over there in Stanhope Place! " pointed Drummond.

The pointsman swung his arm majestically. Cutting across, Fraser manœuvred into a slot facing the park. Drummond swivelled the driving mirror, brushed a hair from his black overcoat. " What about your wife—are you going to phone now ? " he asked casually.

The man's self-control was fantastic. " Yes," said Fraser.

" Then let me go in first," decided Drummond. " I shouldn't be long. If you happen to spot Mrs. Garrett's car, try to get a look inside. There's a slight chance she might have left the dog there." He shut the car door.

Fraser watched Drummond's elegant back across the street. Answering the doorman's salute with a nod, Drummond vanished through the revolving doors.

Fraser waited five minutes then followed. The Bentley was not among the cars parked in the forecourt. He walked past the house cop and quick-eyed receptionists to the telephone alcove. A hard-faced man in uniform sat at the switchboard. The six booths were empty. The chair and table in front of them unoccupied. Fifty yards away from the bustling lobby, there was complete hush here. Fraser dropped a pound note on the switchboard. " When you get this number," he said softly, " I want you to say this is the Landers Clinic."

The man's creased face was unreceptive. He looked at the note suspiciously then folded it into a neat square. " Say it's where ? " he asked. The note was in his hand.

" The Landers Clinic! " Fraser spelled it out. " I'm calling my wife." He looked a little shamefaced. He shrugged. " I'm dining with an old friend. My wife thinks I'm in the Clinic."

" Ah! " the man's voice rose. " I'm very sorry but I couldn't do nothing like that, sir! " He put the money in his pocket. " Two Bridges 26 ? " he asked into the microphone. " This is the Landers Clinic, Ma'am. I have a call for you." He motioned Fraser to a booth.

" I've had the shot, Barby," said Fraser.

Her voice was faint. " I can hardly hear you, darling."

" I've had the shot," he said louder. " I feel great but tired. Listen—Landers is satisfied—I don't have to go back after to-morrow."

She sighed relief. " I'm so glad you called, darling.

I've been waiting in front of the fire seeing nothing but operating theatres and rubber masks. Awful! What are you doing now ? "

" Just going to bed—and you ? " he said.

" Just sitting," she replied. " I've been waiting for your call. Now I think I'll go over to the Gilmours for an hour."

He wanted to hear her laugh. " Is Jim screwed again ? " he asked.

" I don't know. But at least he's civil to Kate if somebody else is there." She sounded as if she wanted to talk on.

He checked his watch. It was 8.15. " I'll have to go, honey," he said suddenly. " They've got my bed ready. I'll be back sometime in the morning. Good-night. I love you." He waited for her whispered answer then hung up.

He dropped a coin to the switchboard. " Never learn, do they, sir ? " the man asked sourly.

" How's that ? " asked Fraser.

The man's mouth drooped, his voice cantankerous. " You're not on your own sir. I get it at home." He puffed indignation. " Where've you bin ? Where you going ? Never a thought you might like a night by yourself—Gawd knows *where* but out ! " He flung a hand at the street. He was suddenly prim. " Good-night, sir."

Fraser crossed the crowded lobby and used the exit by the bar. Cars were parked on the east side of Park Lane for a hundred yards. He walked slowly north. He stopped, recognising Mrs. Garrett's chauffeur. The man was chatting to a group. Fraser cut in front of the Bentley looking into the interior. The car was empty. He waited in the Sunbeam. It was a quarter-hour before Drummond came through the swing doors. He hurried round the corner. Fraser had the door open ready.

Drummond took his seat. His voice was strained " She's there all right. But she's wearing the best part of twenty-thousand pounds. That means we're going to have to wait up for her."

Fraser shifted gloved fingers on the wheel. " How do you mean, wait up for her ? "

Drummond shrugged. " We're not going to leave twenty-thousand pounds behind. We'll have to wait till she goes to sleep. Get it then."

Night and day, he must have played out this last scene a hundred times. The pair of them, stealthily creeping up a silent staircase and into an empty bedroom. He'd pictured himself tense at a window while Drummond opened the safe. Sometimes they ran, a houseful of screaming servants after them. The happiest dream was of a street door closed casually—an unhurried saunter to the waiting car. Now he saw a closed bedroom door. Behind it, a woman who'd heard them move—whispering into a telephone.

He started peeling off his gloves. He shook his head as Drummond started to say something. " I can't do it, I tell you ! " He spoke desperately. " It's been too long—I haven't got the nerve any more."

Drummond's head moved in understanding. " Listen," he said quietly. " I'll open the safe as soon as we're in. When we've got what's there, I'll jam the lock. She'll be able to put her key in—but not to turn it. Try to use your imagination constructively for once," he urged. " She comes home. Up to that point there's nothing to disturb her. She puts her key in the safe—it won't turn. She thinks *she's* jammed it. That leaves only one place for her

115

to put the stuff she's wearing. On the dressing table." He made each point logically. " You don't even have to go in her room. *I'll* get it."

Under the spell of Drummond's certainty, Fraser pulled his gloves on again. He touched the starter. " O.K.," he said huskily. " Where do we go now ? "

" The side entrance of the R.N.V.R. Club," said Drummond.

The car moved north. Fraser braked under the darkened windows of the club offices. Ten yards in front of them, South Street ran east and west. Obliquely to the right was the Garrett house. A light was burning over the steps.

Drummond fished out a pack of cigarettes. " Want a smoke ? It'll be your last chance! " He offered the pack to Fraser.

Fraser cupped gloved hands to take the light. Both men smoked in silence. The smell of charred leather jolted Fraser from his thoughts. He pitched the finished butt through the window.

Drummond pointed at the north side of the street that faced them. " You see the churchyard wall ? "

Fraser nodded. The wall ran along the east side of the intersection, cutting in to South Street at a right angle.

" First thing we've got to do is get the tools into the churchyard. Drive over by the wall and open up the bonnet. Make it look as though you're searching for a loose connection."

Fraser sent the car slowly forward. Right into South Street. Then left again till they flanked the churchyard wall. Drummond signalled a stop. Fraser switched off the motor—got out and put up the hood. As he leaned over the cylinder block he heard people passing on both

116

sides of the street. Lights burned in the church behind
him.

Drummond was out and walking round to the onside
of the car. He opened the door and pulled out the fibre-
glass case. He leaned casually against the side of the car,
watching Fraser pretend to work. Drummond's body
shielded the case on the sidewalk. For a second time
Fraser wrenched off the sparkplug leads and replaced
them. A post office van rounded the corner from South
Street swinging wide to avoid the parked Sunbeam. The
van first slowed then accelerated. As it passed, Drummond
heaved the case over the wall two-handed. There was a
thud then the crash of breaking glass. Drummond
walked round to the front of the car. He leaned his head
under the hood.

" Let's drive back to the Club," he said quietly and
sauntered round to take his seat.

They circled the block. As they passed the Garrett
house the street door and basement area were as bright as
day. The upper windows closed and dark. In the lee of
the club offices, Fraser stopped the car and stilled the
motor.

" It sounded as if you hit a glass factory back there! "
This was short of the easy comment he had hoped for.

Drummond shrugged. " That's because you were
listening for it. You can bet nobody else either saw the
case go or heard it land. Right! " he said suddenly.
" Now we go over ourselves. I'll give you a leg-up."

They walked the length of the wall to the steps at the
church entrance. Drummond's hand steered Fraser to the
right. A heavy curtain hung in front of them. From behind it came the sound of scraping feet, a woman coughing.
Then voices were loud in a hymn.

117

Drummond squatted, head low to the ground, peering out at the sidewalk. He jumped up. " Come on— quick! "

The only pedestrians on the street had their backs to the two men. A dozen yards from the steps Fraser put a foot in Drummond's locked hands and heaved himself up. He flattened his body as he went over the wall. Fingers scraped the brickwork as he fell. Then his heels dug into turf. As he picked himself up, Drummond landed beside him. Pale-haired in the moonlight, Drummond crouched, one hand holding Fraser still. Someone passed by on the other side of the wall.

The churchyard was a rough turfed square. Flagged walks crossed it, affording contemplation of the headstones. A solitary elm, black and bare stood in the centre. The case had landed six feet away. One end in a glass dome protecting wax flowers. Drummond pulled it free of broken fragments. Using the wall as cover, the two men worked their way round the churchyard. When they halted, no more than the wall and a dozen yards separated them from the backs of the South Street houses.

They squatted, the smell of the dank soil in their nostrils. In the church, the organist crashed through major chords to a loud finale.

" Five minutes," whispered Drummond. " Everyone will be gone by then." He nodded at the stained windows. " We may have to use the church door to the street. They always leave one window open in the vestry."

The church lights dimmed one after another. A door banged. They heard someone walking heavily up the street. " That's the vicar," whispered Drummond. He dragged the case to a stone slab and opened it. He looked up, handing Fraser goggles, a pistol. " For God's sake

118

remember there's a safety catch." He pulled on his own goggles, light catching the amber glass. " You don't pull the trigger unless I say so. Is that understood ? "

Fraser nodded. He rammed the weapon as far as it would go in his pocket. Drummond already had the ladder extended the length of three rungs. He signalled Fraser up and followed, hauling the ladder after him. No gardens faced them. There was nothing between the wall and the backs of the houses but a narrow strip of ground covered with dying nettles. The only access to this no-man's-land was over the wall or through a window. Drummond counted the houses—chopped a hand at the third to their right.

They kicked through the nettles, dragging the ladder. Curtains were drawn across the ground-floor windows. Bars spanned the frames. The last yards to the house was hazardous with rusted barbed wire. Drummond pulled a pair of small cutters from his pocket. Bending over the coiled wire, he chopped left and right. With both hands, he wrenched a section of wire from the wall. A space was free to the left of the window, two feet wide. Drummond inched nearer the curtains, his back flat against the wall. Holding the position, he craned towards the window.

He came back to Fraser. " They're eating," he whispered. " They've got the television going but it's out of sight." He dropped the wire cutters in the inside pocket of his overcoat. " The dog's on the cook's lap. The fattest woman I've seen in years! " Overhead, the windows to the servants' bedrooms seemed a hundred yards away. One at each end, they pulled the ladder to its limit. Drummond handled the light frame with ease—walking it to the wall and placing it carefully. The top rung was parallel with the bottom of the window. Drummond

119

heeled pits in the soft earth, plugged them with pebbles. " That'll stop it sinking," he whispered. " I'd better go first. The window may be shut."

Fraser leaned his weight on the ladder as Drummond went up testing each rung carefully. High above, Drummond looked down. He waved and the metal shifted slightly as he took his weight from it. Suddenly he was gone through the open window. After a second, his head showed. He beckoned.

Fraser started up the swaying ladder. Sweating, he tried to put each foot as Drummond had done. Slotted in the angle of strut and rung. Every window he passed was a threat till Drummond hauled him across the sill at the top. Covers glinted on two beds. The room was stuffy with a mixed odour of apples and mothballs. He held Drummond's legs as the blond leaned out, hitching the bottom of the ladder nearer the side of the house.

They stood, immobile, listening. Then Drummond crossed the room and opened the door very slowly. Beyond an open door to their right, an alarm clock ticked noisily. Left was the staircase. The light from the hall filtered up, shedding some of its strength at each landing. Drummond first, they moved down the carpeted stairs without sound, treading close to the wall.

Suddenly, Drummond held up a warning hand. The smell of food drifted up, the muffled sound of music. Ten feet below, the hall was still. Before soft-lit tapestry a few Georgian pieces gleamed, dark and rich. A baize door angled the left-hand corner.

Everything on the second floor was white. The walls, the three doors. One room, the width of the house, over-looked the street.

" That's hers! " mouthed Drummond. He opened the

120

other two doors. Fraser nodded. His throat tickled and he bleated a cough into cupped hands. Drummond shook his head violently, baring his teeth. He gestured at the nearest open door. Fraser had a brief glimpse of a bed then pushed his head into a pillow. He coughed there till the spasm was gone.

" For Crissakes! " whispered Drummond.

Fraser pushed up his mask, wiped his eyes. It was just possible to make out Drummond's shape in the darkened room.

" Both these must be guest rooms," Drummond said softly. His pencil flash picked out the empty dressing-table, the unused beds. He opened an inner door to a connecting bathroom. " Couldn't be better," he whispered. " We've got the run of three rooms." He bent over Fraser. " Think you can control that bloody cough ? "

Fraser nodded again. Drummond's hand was on the door handle. The crack of light widened. " Come on! " he said.

They padded across the landing. Drummond put his ear to the door of the master bedroom. Turning the handle, he stepped back quickly. Satisfied, he waved Fraser in behind him.

" Lock it! " he said. The thin beam held the door as Fraser turned the key. " Window! " said Drummond.

Fraser stood by the heavy damask drapes. The room was warm and sweet-smelling—a refuge from the naked street below. Behind him, the slender shaft of light flickered across the walls, the furnishings. Suddenly he heard Drummond's breath go—and the flat sound of metal on metal. A car's headlamps gave the room brilliance. Drummond was standing in front of an open

121

wall-safe. Fraser forced his eyes back to the street, watching each pedestrian past the portico beneath.

A door banged in the basement. He stepped back as light flooded the area. He kept his eyes on the gate at the top of the basement steps. A woman with a scarf round her head climbed up to the street. Beside her, the dachshund yapped excitedly as she walked off.

Drummond turned. He was holding the leather key bag. Mouth slightly open, he raised his head in question. Fraser motioned safety. He kept his eyes on the woman and dog as they progressed from lamp-post to lamp-post. It must be nearly a quarter to ten, he thought. Pretty soon, all the servants would be going to bed. All except whoever had the chore of waiting up for Mrs. Garrett. He half-swung towards Drummond, remembering the ladder that stood against the wall. It needed no more than one of the maids to look from her window and they were trapped.

Drummond was pushing something into the keyhole of the safe. He snapped the flash off. Fraser heard the door being unlocked. Then Drummond beckoned. They ran up the stairs.

In the servants' room, Drummond sat on a bed and pushed back his mask. " I've got the lot, Kit," he said softly. " Everything except what she's wearing." He dropped the leather bag in an inside pocket. " This ladder's got to be shifted before the maids come up," he whispered. He stood at the window, looking at the quiet churchyard. " We'll collapse it and leave the case in the church." He walked back to the bed and straightened the covers carefully. " Who was that went out ? "

" One of the maids with the dog," Fraser answered. He took off his gloves, wiped his hands, put the gloves on again. He tried to hide his relief. " I think you're dead right not to wait. I never wanted a penny from this deal, Drummond. My share'll make up for whatever you're losing."

Drummond swung suddenly. He came over to stand close to Fraser. " I promised you *two* things," he said quietly. " Nobody's going to bother you and you get an equal share. What you do with it afterwards is your business. But you *get* it."

Fraser moved hesitantly to the window. Drummond's voice stopped him. " You're not going down that ladder, Kit. Only me." He took off his goggles. " Hold these for me and wait in Mrs. Garrett's room till I'm back."

The street door slammed. Both men tiptoed to the landing. The maid was kneeling in the hall, unfastening the dog's collar. Drummond led the way back. " There's only one lock being used—the Ingersoll. It'll be like that till she gets back." He grabbed Fraser by the shoulders. " I'll be fifteen minutes at the most. Don't move from her window. When you see me turn the corner into South Street, get down and unlock that door." His fingers dug into Fraser's flesh.

He went through the window backwards, legs dangling till his feet found the ladder rungs. He took his weight on his palms, flat against the brickwork. " Fifteen minutes," he repeated.

Fraser watched as Drummond pulled away the ladder and collapsed it. The blond clambered over the church wall. He ran swiftly over the flagged paths, turning to wave from the shadow of the elm. Then he was gone.

Fraser considered the twenty-foot drop to the ground. Even if he hung from the sill he might finish in the nettles with a broken ankle. He crept out to the landing. The old fear was back with renewed intensity. This had the smell of a trap. Drummond with the bulk of the loot—for all he knew, the lot! Suppose Drummond didn't intend to come back! Suppose he'd been left to tell the cops a story no-one would believe.

Dry-lipped, he picked his way downstairs. It couldn't be. Kline was capable of pulling a thing like that but not Drummond. Fifteen minutes, Drummond had promised. O.K., he'd wait thirty. A half-hour was fair—if Drummond hadn't shown by then . . . . Down on the second floor, the noise of the television set was louder. The maids were shrieking with laughter. He opened Mrs. Garrett's bedroom and locked the door behind him. Then stood stock-still. Someone had turned on a heater—the bed had been folded down. Shocked, he took his place by the window. If anyone came to the door, it would take only seconds to release the catch. The drop to the street was nothing. Ten feet only to the top step. On each side of the window frame was a small metal box bearing the word TECTATHIEF.

He looked for the switch that controlled the beam. Groping desperately behind curtains, under the dressing-table. It was probably downstairs. One of the maids had the job of setting and releasing it. The moment he went through that window, Savile Row Police Station would erupt. He imagined a cop droning into the police transmitter. In the vehicles, the men crouching with headsets, directing their drivers. The scream of tyres as the cars converged on the lighted doorway below.

He checked his watch. Already twelve minutes had gone. As he looked up, Drummond came round the corner. He was walking easily, arms swinging. Nobody was following him.

Fraser unlocked the door to the landing. The baize door below seemed greener, bigger. He took the twelve stairs quickly. Unable to prevent himself, he crossed the hall and listened at the green baize. Then hurrying to the street door he pulled the catch. Drummond slipped in quickly. Once inside, he exploded into a series of swift movements. He bent down, scanning the locks not used, the bolts. Opened the door again and shut it. A streak of dirt was across one cheek. " Up! " he mouthed. They hurried up to the guest room.

They sat whispering in the darkness. " We ought to be able to see the hall from here," said Drummond suddenly. At the door, he pulled out the key and squatted. The bed creaked as he sat down again. " Just the top of the stairs, no more."

The windows faced the side of the neighbouring house. A light came and went there. " The maids'll be up in a couple of minutes," said Fraser. " You've got this door locked."

Drummond shifted impatiently. " You said her bed's been turned down—that's all they're doing for the night. Maids don't go poking about unused rooms at half-past ten." His hand tapped Fraser's pockets. " Where's your pistol? "

Fraser dug deep. He held the squat weapon uncomfortably.

" Here," he said.

" If anyone tries this door—I'm opening it. As soon as I do, pull your trigger," Drummond said evenly. " We go out the front way, in a hurry."

They waited in silence, Drummond flitting from door to bed to window and back. I'm going to tell him to sit down when he gets to the door this time, Fraser thought.

Instead he watched, leaning towards the sound of each passing car.

Drummond's padding came to a sudden halt. The slender disc of light from the keyhole was blocked as he bent. The women's voices grew louder. Footsteps sounded outside. Someone opened the door to Mrs. Garrett's room. After a moment it was shut again. Footsteps started to climb the staircase.

" Two of 'em Kit." Drummond's hand found Fraser's shoulder. " The fat cook and somebody else." He shone the tiny flash on his watch. " Eighteen minutes past eleven. The dog's down there with the maid who's left."

They sat till midnight sounded from a half-dozen churches. Suddenly the dog started barking. Fraser was off the bed. Drummond pushed him back, opened the door slightly. Voices sounded in the hall. A man's voice, quiet, respectful. Then Mrs. Garrett making no concession to the hour. " Down, Andy —*down*! Has he been out ? " The maid's reply was lost in the movement.

" Take him as far as the garage," said Mrs. Garrett. " It'll be a run for him." The man answered her. As she started to cross the hall, Drummond quietly closed the door. Her voice was muffled but still plain. " He'd better sleep downstairs to-night, Abbott. And don't disturb me in the morning. I'll ring when I'm ready for breakfast."

Fraser pulled back the safety-catch. Take one each, Drummond had said—aim at the face and hold your breath. He put the pistol back in his pocket.

Mrs. Garrett was at her bedroom door. They heard the maid go in after her—water was running in Mrs. Garrett's bathroom. As the maid left the room, the key turned in the lock.

Drummond waited five minutes before peering out at the landing. The lights were still burning in the hall. Fraser put his ear against the dividing wall. A foot away, Mrs. Garrett splashed in her bath.

Drummond nodded across the landing. " She's locked herself in." Fraser nodded back. He mimed someone washing, pointing at the wall in front of him. The dog would sleep downstairs, she'd said. Where . . . on a cushion in the hall maybe—to come to life with the first move that they made.

Someone was climbing the steps from the street to the front door. Once more they waited in darkness. Minutes passed then a stair tread creaked under the chauffeur's weight. Drummond bent at the keyhole. " All the lights are out, now," he whispered. " They've left the dog in the kitchen."

Mrs. Garrett's bedroom was locked, Fraser thought. Unless she unfastened it before going to bed, the expertise involved in opening it was as delicate and precise as that of a good dentist. Drummond's flash searched the writing-desk. He upended the empty cut glass vase—put it to the wall, using it as a sounding bell. He came back to the bed. " I'll give her an hour," he said softly. He left the door to the dark landing open. The house was completely still. Like some quiet fortress, where people slept secure in their defence. Occasionally a board creaked. A clock chimed. Once the motor whirred in the air-conditioning unit. All were familiar sounds accepted subconsciously by those who slept.

Fraser's mouth was dry, his hands wet. The goggles cut into the flesh under his eyes. Drummond checked his watch periodically. To Fraser time seemed to stand still. Suddenly he felt Drummond move on the bed beside him.

He took the proffered flashlight—held it as Drummond
opened and shut the barrel-nosed forceps. " O.K.,"
whispered Drummond. " I'm going in." On the landing
he brought his mouth close to Fraser's ear. " If you hear
me shout, get that front door open as quickly as you can."
He forced Fraser down on the top stair. " Don't move
otherwise. If you hear somebody coming . . ." he
crooked his index finger.

Drummond tiptoed to the door of Mrs. Garrett's bedroom. The pencil flash held in his teeth—forceps in his
hand. Behind the white silk handkerchief in his overcoat
breast pocket, the butt of his pistol showed. He stood still
for a second, listening. Then bent his head, playing the
beam on the keyhole. The end of the key barrel pro-
truded an eighth of an inch on the outside. He fitted the
nose of the forceps round it. Though he seemed to squeeze
gently, his gloved hands shook with the intensity of his
grip. Very slowly, he turned his wrists clockwise. Still
without haste, he pocketed the instrument.

Wiping the sweat from his face, he opened the door.
He glided into the room with the silence of a trained
nurse.

Fraser sat on the staircase, staring into the darkness.
He'd checked the catch on his pistol so often he no longer
knew if it was on or off. Fascinated, he craned back at the
open bedroom door. The tiny flash moved from dressing
table to wall and bed, hovering like a firefly. He willed
Drummond from the room—blocking his ears against the
scream he felt must follow.

Suddenly Drummond stood in the doorway. Under
the goggle mask his mouth was smiling. He beckoned.
Something stronger than fear took Fraser to the door.
He followed the flickering light to the pillow. Mrs.

Garrett lay on her back, her mouth sagging—sound of her snores filled the room.

"Everything," mouthed Drummond touching his pocket. He took the key and locked the door from the outside. Then dropped the key in his pocket. "That'll give 'em something to think about," he said with satisfaction. He spent a minute in the room where they'd waited, straightening bed covers, rugs. He shut the door. "Come on," he said. "Out!"

They ran down the staircase without sound. The street door was bolted. Drummond had the top bolt off when the dog started barking down below. They heard the animal's paws scrabbling at the baize door across the darkened hall. The bottom bolt—the two Bramah locks. And suddenly, the cold night air was in their faces. As he shut the street door behind him, Fraser thought he heard a woman's voice call. The street was empty. They sprinted the seventy-five yards to the parked Sunbeam. Drummond stuffed goggles and guns under the back seat. "Quick—the church," he ordered.

Fraser slammed the car into gear. As they crossed South Street the lights came on in the Garrett house. Drummond had the door open. "Keep her running." He ran up the church steps—came back carrying the fibre-glass suitcase.

He settled back in his seat, turning up his coat collar. "Wilton Place. I'll tell you if anyone's on our tail. With any luck we'll beat the first lot of squad cars." Fraser swung the car west into Upper Grosvenor Street and Drummond added: "Once past Hyde Park Corner, we're all right."

The traffic lights were with them at Hamilton Place. Fraser tucked the Sunbeam behind a cab making the

129

sweep round to Knightsbridge. As they passed the arch, the lighted clock showed eleven minutes past one. He felt Drummond's foot touch his. A black police car screeched east in the opposite direction. Drummond swung round to watch it. " Park Lane," he said. " They don't lose any time."

Thirty yards south on Wilton Place, Fraser pulled the Sunbeam into the cul-de-sac facing the church. Drummond's Jaguar was last in the row of parked cars. The blond flipped the lid of the second suitcase. " Get out of those things," he instructed. He threw slacks, shoes, a leather jacket at Fraser.

The two men changed quickly. The moon was still bright and threw sharp shadows. In the church tower wheels ground and whirred. The clock banged the half-hour on a cracked bell. In a cashmere sweater and slacks, Drummond was slimmer—less sinister. He scratched the back of his neck, yawning. " I've got eleven miles to go to dump this lot." He flapped a hand at the car and contents. " *And* take a chance on how I get home."

Fraser couldn't get Barby out of his mind. She'd be sleeping—the moonlight at the head of her bed as it had been two nights before. That's all he wanted, he thought. To be back with her, the last week forgotten. Yet it could never be like that. This might be the end for the other two—for *him* it was only the beginning. Unless he refused Patterson's offer of a partnership, he'd live the lie for the rest of his life. That was it, he had to get away—leave England with Barby. Start all over again. This time on his own terms.

When he looked up, Drummond was watching him. The blond shook his head. " In a month's time, you'll have forgotten all about it," he said tolerantly. His face was friendly. " So will I. I'll be on your side of the fence, Kit. My God, I may even pay taxes." He grinned. " That's a problem for you—how are you going to declare your windfall ? Capital gains ? "

Till the time for the final refusal, discussion was useless. Not till then would Drummond believe he was being anything but coy about his share in the loot. " I suppose you know what you're doing," he said slowly. " Me—I don't trust Kline out of grabbing range."

Drummond sank back in his seat as a pair of uniformed cops strolled past the end of the cul-de-sac. Their footsteps died away.

Drummond considered what he had said. " Kline's been a necessary part of this scheme. Without him, the stuff could never have been sold with safety."

" If you don't trust Kline . . ." Fraser started.

" When I'm sure I like to be certain," said Drummond. " I'd be happier if I knew why Kline offered you that bed," he said.

Fraser shrugged. " To keep me off the streets, I suppose. Have me where he could see what I was up to—I thought it was your idea as much as his! "

Drummond shook his head. " A hotel room would have kept you off the streets. And Kline's as sure of you by now as I am. It's more than that—you could help me find out how *much* more."

He told himself he owed Drummond nothing. What he had contracted to do was done. " What sort of help ? " he asked guardedly.

Drummond was quick to explain. " Kline's got a meeting with the buyer at eight in the morning. He's paid as soon as the bank vaults are open—that's ten o'clock. Will you phone me as soon as he leaves the flat ? "

131

" Why ? " asked Fraser.

Drummond lit a cigarette blew the answer with the smoke. " I know the bank he's going to. I'm going to make sure he gets back to the flat safely."

Fraser shrugged. " O.K. Where ? " Drummond gave him a number. He hefted the bag of jewellery. For a moment, he seemed about to add something. His mouth was twisted wryly.

" Take these to the master-mind," he said at last. " Don't forget, if you lose them we're all in trouble."

He groped under the bumper of the Jaguar. Car keys were scotch-taped to the metal. He handed them to Fraser. " I'll be waiting," he said.

Fraser put the grey car in gear. " I'll phone you." As he turned into Wilton Place, he saw the Sunbeam being backed out.

He drove carefully. Halting for lights that flashed across empty streets as if for him alone. At Sloane Street he turned south. As he reached the K.L.M. terminal, a car came up fast behind him. Somehow he managed to keep his eyes on the road ahead. He had a blurred impression of peering heads as the police car passed. Braking violently, the driver turned off towards Lowndes Square.

He waited for the lights at Pont Street. The street was empty and he had the certainty that he was beyond the dragnet. The forecourt of the apartment building was alight. A porter at the door turned his head curiously as Fraser drove down the ramp. He left the Jaguar parked in front of the tenants garages.

The shoes Drummond had given him made no sound as he climbed back up the concrete slope. He looked through the glass pane in the service door. Passage and lobby were empty. He pushed the door open and locked the bar in place. His finger was barely off the door button when Kline opened. He followed Fraser into the sitting room.

Kline's robe showed a mat of grey hair on his chest. His feet were stuffed into heelless slippers. Windows were shut tight and the room harboured the stink of Kline's cigarettes. The ash tray on the centre table was filled with butts. Kline braced himself in front of Fraser's chair. " Well ? " he asked anxiously.

Very slowly Fraser pulled the bag from his pocket. He tossed it on the table. Kline's fingers flexed like those of a man who tries new gloves. He picked up the bag, making every movement with deliberation. " Splendid," he said softly. He spread a black velvet square on the table, set a jeweller's lupe and a handful of implements by its side. " *Now*! " he said smiling and emptied the bag on the velvet square.

Fraser watched, fascinated, as Kline lined the pieces in front of him. Months before, he'd sat with Mrs. Garrett in a double-locked office as the Underwriters' valuer appraised the collection. He recognized each piece as Kline checked it against his list. Bar and clip brooches. A collar and tiara. Three bracelets and a necklace. The eighteen-carat solitaire. These were no semi-precious or coloured stones, only gem quality diamonds.

Kline was lost to everything but the jewellery. The lupe in his eye, he weighed and inspected. Sensitive fingers, black-fuzzed to the first knuckle, rotated each piece. Once he seemed to sniff the setting. Another time he used the tip of his tongue on a diamond's facet. Suddenly he hooked his feet under the chair rung and sat up straight.

" Beautiful," he said reverently. He swung his head almost belligerently at Fraser. " Don't you *see* how

beautiful it is ? " he asked. He threw an Empire pin to
Fraser's lap. His lower lip stuck out, daring criticism.

Fraser took the pin in his hand. It was old, certainly.
And French. A court jeweller's conception of a sunburst
wrought in a hundred brilliants. Yet, like the rest of the
jewels, it had no meaning for him. He rubbed smarting
eyes, remembering Drummond miles away. Caught up
in God knows what derring-do to seal his plan with
perfection. He threw the pin back on the table, yawning
indifferently. As Kline shook his head Fraser snarled in
sudden anger. " You don't want to know what happened
in that house! All you're interested in is getting your
hands on that jewellery." It was hot in the room. He
threw his suède jacket to the sofa. On an impulse, he
grabbed the velvet square, the jewels hard against his
palm. He stood facing the lawyer across the table. " You
haven't a thought for me—for Drummond. Only for
this! " He let the bundle drop under Kline's nose.

The lawyer seized the square—opened it solicitously.

" You can chip five hundred pounds from a stone like
that," he reproved. He looked up, bland-eyed. Then the
corners of his mouth lifted. " I didn't have to worry with
you and Mark on the job. Pour yourself a drink, for God's
sake, Kit. And stop being intense." Fraser took the
bottle and Kline went back to his inspection. Suddenly
his eyebrow leaped. He caught the falling lupe handily.
" You got everything! " he said softly.

" Everything," repeated Fraser.

Kline's two hands cupped the piled jewels. He nodded
to himself. " Wasn't she wearing any jewellery! "

Fraser emptied his glass. Kline's menace was gone.
The man was no more than a bare-shanked, evil old
buzzard.

" She was and it's there. Down to the last gramme. Where do I sleep ? "

Kline jerked his head at the sofa behind him. " On that. It opens up to a bed. You'll find blankets and sheets in the linen closet by the bathroom."

As Fraser made the bed, Kline cut all lights but a reading lamp on the table. Putting the lupe back in his eye, he picked up the solitaire. He used tiny forceps expertly, twisting the claws that held the giant stone in its setting. The loose diamond flashed in his palm. He weighed it on a jeweller's balance. Sighing gently, he started to break up the tiara.

In the bathroom, Fraser scrubbed his mouth clean with the corner of a towel. Through the open window, the whole building seemed to sleep. The only light was in the corridor three feet across the angle of the wall. He went back to the stuffy room and lay down watching Kline through half-open eyes. It was past two before the lawyer had finished. The pile of loose diamonds had been sorted into small parcels. Each was wrapped in blue tissue paper. All that remained of jewellers' artistry was a heap of gold and platinum mountings. Kline held the metal fragments in his palms. He forced his hands together as though crushing walnuts. Humming, he chopped the remainder to bits with a pair of pliers.

He yawned, scratching the hair on his chest. As he turned, Fraser shut his eyes quickly, feigning sleep. He felt the lawyer's breath as the man leaned over the sofa.

" Kit! " whispered Kline. Fraser stirred. " Good night," smiled Kline. " Get some sleep—we've got to be up early."

When the bedroom door shut, Fraser drew shades and opened windows. The church across the street was the

135

colour of birch bark in the moonlight. He shivered as the frosty air hit his bare skin. As he climbed into bed, the key turned in the bedroom door.

He awoke troubled and confused. Expecting to see the familiar outline of Barby's bed, he rolled over. It was still dark outside but a light showed under the bottom of the kitchen door. He sat on the side of the sofa, holding his head in his hands, remembering. He looked at his watch as the kitchen door opened. It was half-past six.

Kline was carrying a tea tray. He had shaved and washed and smelled of lotions. A foulard scarf tucked into the neckline of his robe hid the hair on his chest. He gave Fraser a cup and sat on the other side of the table, sipping his tea noisily.

The brew was strong and hot. From behind the rim of his cup, he watched Kline cautiously. For all the lawyer's spruceness he looked tired. His eyes had black hollows. As if he'd sat up all night, watching the loot, thought Fraser. Once again he'd been wrong about the man across the table. The evil was back in the spread of the heavy shoulders—the deceptive mildness in Kline's voice.

" You slept soundly, Kit. I've been up for a half-hour. Not a move from you as I came through." He seemed pleased with himself. " I hope you rested—there's a lot to do."

Fraser pushed the cup away, started pulling on his trousers. Kline rapped a nail on the table, calling Fraser's attention.

" Still a lot to do," he repeated.

" Not for me, there isn't," said Fraser. " Is there any more tea ? " When his cup had been filled, he settled his back against the sofa. " I'm getting home as fast as I can."

" Not yet, Kit," said Kline.

136

The tone dragged him back over years to the cells beneath the Old Bailey. To the long walk along a clanging corridor—the bare room where Kline waited. The lawyer's eyes had been bird-bright as they were now—his voice hushed and gentle.

Fraser's mind raced over the possibility of fresh treachery. " How do you mean, not yet ? " he asked guardedly.

Kline shrugged into a comfortable position. The electric heater at his feet was buzzing. He kicked the switch without taking his eyes from Fraser.

" There's some more driving for you to do this morning."

Fraser shrugged uneasily. The cigarette on an empty stomach had an evil taste. He walked past Kline and bundled the bedding into the linen closet. The wire recording was safely on its way to Two Bridges by now. For a moment he thought of shocking Kline with the disclosure but swallowed the threat. The lawyer probably wanted to be chauffeured to his appointment—to the bank —afterwards.

In the bathroom he put his head in a basin of cold water. The stubbled face in the mirror was red-eyed. Like that of a drunk, he thouhgt, on his way to Magistrates' Court. He had to borrow Kline's razor. He opened the small cabinet. The electric razor that had been there the night before was gone.

He walked back to the living-room. Kline's door was half shut. There was a bowl of fruit on the table. Fraser stood at the window, peeling a banana.

" What car are we going to use ? " he asked casually.

Kline's bulk filled the doorway. " Mark's, I think. It's outside. There's no time to go chasing up to Park Lane for yours." He was wearing a light grey suit, black

137

knitted tie and sober shoes. He came into the living-room, pulling the door shut behind him.

" I'll have to call my wife first," said Fraser.

Kline waved his hand at the telephone on the spinet. " By all means. Say you'll be back this afternoon." He glanced at his watch. " Seven-thirty. Will your wife be awake ? "

Fraser gave his words the right amount of concern. " She thinks I'm lying," he said steadily. " She doesn't think I spent the night in that clinic."

Kline lowered himself to the sofa, head tilted. " Ahah! " His voice was soft. " Then what ? "

Fraser hunched his shoulders. " Who the hell knows— maybe with some other woman. When I called her last night, she just wouldn't listen. It could be different this morning. At any rate, once she knows I'm on my way home, she'll figure the argument can keep." He looked down at the street. It was almost daybreak. Already people were hurrying to work.

" If she's tried to get in touch with me, God knows the answer."

Kline worried the quick of his thumbnail. " Nobody called here last night. I never moved from the flat." He looped the extension cord and carried the phone to the window. " Phone her now," he ordered. " Tell her you finish with the doctor this morning. You'll come straight home then."

Fraser made no move to pick up the instrument. " I told you she thinks I'm lying. She's capable of getting the exchange to check this number. I've done my part in all this," he urged. " I don't want a hysterical woman here on my hands."

Kline rammed the mouthpiece back in its cradle.

138

" Then for Chrissakes, go out and phone her. There's a box at the corner. And hurry back. Time's getting short." He held the front door ajar, peeping into the corridor. " Use the side exit. You look like a tramp."

Left and right, along the stretch of carpet, the apartments were stirring. The smell of frying bacon pervaded the corridor. Sound of a radio came from behind closed doors. As he passed one mail box, an invisible hand snatched the newspapers from it. He went through the pass door, buttoning the suède jacket to the neck. It would be too early for the account of the robbery to be in the papers. For some obscure reason he wanted to be with Barby when she heard.

He stepped out into the lower passage. The side door was no more than a dozen feet away. He had his hand on the bar to raise it when a voice echoed along the corridor. " H-e-y! " He turned. A porter was running towards him from the lobby. " Just a minute! " the man called.

Fraser walked back to meet him. The porter was shortish—dressed in the brown livery of the building. His face had been scraped to shining redness. He looked both zealous and alert.

" Good morning," said Fraser. The porter made no reply.

In the lobby, a squad of charwomen was attacking floor and windows. A second porter watched the women, sucking his teeth with melancholy. He came over as the short one called. The two men turned in on Fraser, flanking him. He was suddenly conscious of his beard—his general air of raffishness. He shifted feet, looking from one to the other. " Well ? " he invited.

" You're not a tenant here, are you ? " The short man seemed to consider the word " sir " then dismissed it.

139

" That ain't the way out! " added the second. He wore ribbons on his chest and took himself seriously. He eased round to get between Fraser and the revolving doors.

Fraser stepped back. He knew how he should handle these oafs but the back of his neck was red. Fear and urgency hampered his judgment. " I know the way out," he said shortly. " Suppose you two sleuths get about your business."

Both tone and accent bothered the short man. But he stood his ground. " This *is* our business. We're paid to know who goes in and out of this-here building."

Across the lobby, the four women had stopped. Mops and vacuums forgotten, they waited for every word expectantly. The man with the ribbons sucked in air and blew it out pompously. At that hour, the smell of beer was unpleasant. " We got a right to ask 'oo you are and where you just come from," he said portentously. " Creeping in and out the building, eight o'clock in the morning."

The man was right and time going. " I stayed with Mr. Kline last night," said Fraser patiently. " Number thirty-nine. I'm going out for five minutes. If it's all right with you, I'll be coming back again."

The man with the ribbons swung on the giggling chars. The vacuums droned. The short porter was slightly discomfited, but he was dogged as well. " Mr. Kline ? We've got orders about Mr. Kline. He's away. Be away a twelve-month." He was backing towards the desk and the telephone.

" Why don't you ask him if he's there ? " said Fraser sarcastically.

The man took the house phone—spoke for a couple of minutes. He turned to Fraser, his face strained with un-

140

willing apology. " Sorry, sir. But we've got our instructions. Stands to reason in a place like this." He was
watching Fraser curiously, taking in every detail of
clothes and appearance.

The ex-soldier spun the revolving door for Fraser's
benefit. Ignoring both of them, Fraser walked back the
length of the corridor, leaving the building by the side
entrance.

Outside, he looked up at Kline's windows, unable to
resist the urge. There was no one there. He broke into a
trot that took him as far as the empty booth.

Drummond's number rang without answer. Fraser
thumbed the button—put the coins back in the box. He
had to be there! Fraser read the scrap of paper again and
redialled. The earpiece clicked and Drummond's voice
sounded wearily.

" We're just leaving the building," said Fraser.
" Kline says I've got to drive him. In your car."

" Where ? "

Fraser shrugged. " I don't know. You said he had an
appointment at eight."

Drummond was thoroughly awake now. " He'd never
let you within a mile of it. Listen . . ." he seemed to
ponder.

In the small square of mirror, Fraser's forehead was
dirty and sweating. " What ? " he asked.

" Is there anything you've noticed about him—anything odd ? "

Fraser stared at his reflection. He had to shave before
he saw Barby. The razor! Memory added the score.
" His razor's gone from the bathroom," he burst out.
" And the porters seem to think he's leaving."

Drummond's voice came and went as if he were dressing

141

already. " I'm coming over right away. Can you leave the front door open ? "

Fraser shook his head. " You know Kline."

Drummond's voice was sharp. " Then get it open as soon as you hear the chime. No matter what, get that door open! "

His hand shook as he put down the receiver. He found more coins and called Two Bridges. The early morning workers were passing in streams now. No worries, he thought. Not a single one of them with a real worry. No more than a job and a day that might bore them.

Barby's voice answered anxious and inquiring.

" Thank God you phoned, darling. I was just going to ring the clinic."

Somebody had pasted a sticker on the side of the coin box. He picked it off mechanically. THE WAGES OF SIN IS DEATH.

" I don't think I'm going to be able to make it before this afternoon," he said slowly. " Early afternoon," he promised.

She broke in quickly. " That's what I was going to call you about, Kit. Daddy was on the phone a half-hour ago. He wants you to go straight to the office."

" The office! " he repeated. " What's he want me there for ? " He was sweating. In spite of the frost outside, the booth was hot.

" That woman was robbed last night." She gave him the news almost casually.

From police to insurance company before eight o'clock was quick work. He wanted to be off the street—back in Kline's apartment with Drummond there. With Drummond he felt safer. " What woman ? " he asked.

" Mrs. Garrett," said Barby. " She rang Daddy at

142

home. At three this morning. Apparently she's almost off her head. Daddy wants you to meet him at Suffolk Street, as soon as you can after ten."

" Call him back," he said slowly. " Call him back and say I'll get there as soon as I can."

" You sound strange," she said suddenly. " Are you sure you're feeling well ? "

" I'm fine. Everything's fine, Barby," he said vaguely. " I'll come straight home from the office."

Heedless of the stares, he jogged back to the apartment building. The side entrance was shut. Somebody had raised the bar inside. He walked round to the front of the building. The short porter took the elevator up to the third floor. He opened the gate with a gesture. " Thirty-nine's on your right, sir," he said poker-faced.

Fraser followed Kline into the living-room. A cashmere coat hid the lawyer's grey suit. He was wearing thick-framed spectacles.

" You were long enough about it," he complained. Kline put his wife's photograph in the black brief-case. His voice sounded casual enough. He had his back turned, searching the top of the spinet, tearing up some papers, pocketing others.

Fraser sat on the end of the sofa. He undid the suède jacket. " She took a lot of convincing."

The last of the documents dealt with, Kline dropped the ripped papers in the empty fruit bowl and set fire to them.

" As long as you shut her up," he said shortly.

Fraser shrugged. " I'll find out whether I've shut her up when I get home. Not before." The papers in the bowl were smouldering. Both men wiped their eyes.

" How about letting me use your razor ? " asked Fraser. He touched the stubble on his face. " You're right when

143

you say I look like a tramp. It was a near thing whether or not the porters called the cops."

Kline hesitated, then pulled the electric razor from his brief-case. " You've got five minutes."

Fraser plugged in and started to clean the beard from his cheeks. He had only the vaguest idea where Drummond lived. The number he'd called had been a Flaxman exchange. That meant Chelsea. Drummond's car was downstairs and cabs hard to find at this hour of the morning.

The room was still acrid with the smell of burning paper. Kline opened both windows. As cold air swept in, he shivered. Buttoning his overcoat, he switched on the electric fire. Fraser was standing as near as he could to the front door. He moved the full length of the razor's flex. One cheek was already smooth. The whine of the elevator came clear above the sound of the tiny motor.

Kline leaned his back against the window, his lips pursed in a flat tuneless whistle. " I get the same satisfaction from this as I did in the old days. Taking a case to the Appeal Court and winning it," he said. " First the logical plan then its implementation. Do you know what I mean, Kit ? "

The man's voice was friendly—almost confiding. The elevator gates clanged along the corridor. Surely Kline must hear them. Fraser's voice was unnecessarily loud. He half turned in the open doorway. " You're talking in riddles."

Kline raised both eyebrows. " It's quite simple. I told you I'd be leaving England when this was over. I'm going on a long trip, Kit. And all interested parties will be either jubilant or indifferent." He shut the window. " Except one."

Fraser moved with the first chime. The razor fell and spun on the polished boards buzzing like an angry wasp. Fraser jerked the door open and slammed it shut behind Drummond. Kline had followed him into the hall. As the two men came towards him, he backed slowly.

Drummond's mac was belted over a pyjama top. His pale shining hair neat. Kline's face showed no colour at all. His palms found the wall behind him. Drummond kicked the living-room door shut. Fraser bent down and silenced the spinning razor.

" You're early, Mark! " Kline said nervously. His eyes sought a lead first from Fraser then Drummond. He held up a hand, somehow managing a smile. " Kit's driving me to the buyer's."

Drummond stood in the centre of the room. Without taking his eyes from Kline, he walked over to the bedroom door—jerked it open. Two packed suitcases stood by the bed. As the lawyer turned, Drummond jumped him with a half-nelson. The upper part of Kline's body bent backwards under pressure. Suddenly the two struggling men were on the floor. Kline's head was still locked in the stranglehold.

" His pockets," gasped Drummond.

Fraser ripped out papers, ticket folder and passport. Kline's spectacles had shattered against a chair leg. Eyes half-closed, he was pawing feebly. One after another, Fraser searched the pockets. Something moved beneath the lawyer's shirt. Fraser tore it open. The leather bag hung suspended by a cord from the lawyer's neck. Both men stepped over Kline to the table. Drummond pulled a handful of blue paper packets from the bag. He opened four or five. " Get up," he said quietly.

Kline climbed up labouriously. He kneaded his

145

bruised throat. " You're insane," he croaked. He bent
to pick up the broken spectacles. " If you'll let me explain . . ." he looked past Drummond to Fraser. " Trust
him and we're all sunk, Mark," he urged. " I never knew
till late last night but he's been acting under police
instructions from the beginning! "

Drummond swung the bag deliberately. Left then
right. Blood welled from the corner of Kline's cut lip.
" You bastard," said Drummond with feeling.

Fraser recovered ticket and passport. He read aloud:
" El Salvador. First Class flight. One way."

Drummond took the voucher. " Ten-twenty this
morning. That's where you were going to drive him—the
airport. There wasn't any buyer—no trip to the bank."

Kline leaned against the spinet, dabbing his mouth
ineffectually. " Let me go, Mark," he pleaded. " With
no more than one decent-size stone."

" I'm going to see that you go," said Drummond
suddenly. " But you go with what's in your pockets.
Nothing more. If you ever come back to England, I'll
have a surprise waiting for you."

Kline's hand slid under the spinet top. It came up
holding a nickel-plated revolver. He wiped blood on the
backs of his fingers.

" Give me the bag, Mark," he said unsteadily. " And
the ticket and passport." He stretched out his free hand.
Fraser gulped. He was near enough to the gun to see the
nickel-plated bullet ends in the cylinder. Kline was
watching Drummond. The blond had not altered his
position. He grinned. " Drama! " he said contemptuously. " Put it away, Kline. We know one another too
well."

As Drummond spoke, Fraser drove at Kline's legs. The

gun wavered and Drummond sprang, arms outstretched. The shot reverberated round the closed room. Drummond seemed to reach up, stumbling against Fraser then fell heavily on his face. Fraser knew he was saying something—he wanted Drummond to get up. He hauled the blond man over. The shot had taken Drummond a fraction above the left eye. His mouth sagged—his nostrils dribbled blood. Fraser touched both wrists then lowered on ear against Drummond's chest. For the first time since the shot, he looked up at Kline.

The lawyer's face was expressionless. He was having difficulty with his words. " Throw the bag over, Kit," he whispered. He pushed the pistol a fraction in Fraser's direction.

Fraser threw the bag across the carpet. " He's dead," he said flatly.

Kline pocketed bag, passport and ticket. " You bloody fool! " His voice was shaking. Gun in his back, Fraser walked to the bathroom. Kline found a roll of adhesive tape. He marched Fraser back to the living-room. " Face down on the floor—arms behind your back," the lawyer ordered.

He went down slowly. He could no longer think. For the moment he was almost glad to be told what he must do. Tape locked both wrists in the small of his back. Next his ankles were fastened. There was the sound of ripping material. The lawyer knotted strips round Fraser's hands, hauled its length over Fraser's shoulders and between his legs. Fastened the free end to the bound wrists. He knelt down, testing the strength of the bonds. He searched Fraser's pockets, mumbling between wheezing gasps. He left nothing—taking the keys to the Jaguar, Fraser's money.

He bent away, looking at Drummond's body. A patch of blood was spreading, seeping into the carpet. Kline brought a rubber mat from the bathroom and placed it under Drummond's head. He stepped back to inspect the two prostrate figures. Fraser put the whole force of his lungs into one loud shout. As he strained for the second yell, Kline rammed a balled handkerchief into his mouth. Lodging the linen between Fraser's teeth, he strapped it firmly with tape. Next came a crisscross of plaster that covered Fraser's eyes.

Somebody rapped on the door then the chimes sounded. Fraser heard Kline walk to the hall, the door close. A woman's voice was curious. Then Kline's familiar boom, reassuring. Fraser's scream was no more than a muffled groan that tortured his eardrums. No light penetrated his taped eyelids. He could neither see, speak nor move. Only hear.

A board in the bedroom creaked. Kline was closing windows. The switch clicked as the lawyer turned off the fire. Suddenly Fraser sensed Kline standing over him. He braced himself against the unknown. The front door opened and shut. He heard Kline fastening the Bramah locks. Fraser counted till he heard the elevator gate slam. The apartment was completely quiet.

He lay like a blinded and half-trussed hen, fighting the growing terror. The handkerchief in his mouth was already sodden. The effort to shout through the gag had brought it back nearer his throat. If he panicked, he choked. He was on his back. The weight of his body deadened all feeling in his arms. He heaved twice and rolled over on his face. The soggy ball no longer clogged his gullet. He worked the handkerchief with his tongue. Then rolled over again—and again—trying to weaken the tape. His skin stretched, but the tape held. Suddenly his knees touched something yielding. Drummond.

He lay still for a long while, recreating the room in his mind. To his right was the spinet—the door to the hall-way. To his left, the sofa and Kline's bedroom. Beyond, the kitchen. There'd be knives in the drawers if he could roll as far. And if the door were shut . . . how would he manage the handle. He couldn't even get off the floor. Then something to rub against—something sharp. Even a blunt piece of metal. Drummond's legs sagged as Fraser rolled over them. The fire! If he could only reach the fire! Wriggling desperately, he freed himself from the table-legs. Using belly and knees, he inched towards the wall till he felt the skirting. Keeping his scalp against the wood, he explored to the right. Nothing. He reversed the movement. The flex ran into its socket, six inches away. He pushed his face over the switch and jerked his head down. Every trapped part of his body wanted to function. He wasn't getting enough air through his nostrils. He felt the heat from the fire and crawled towards it—toppled it with his knee. He wriggled the small of his back on to the fire. As the warmth reached the bare skin on his wrists, he bore down, pushing between the guard struts. Tears trickled through the tape to spill on his neck.

He bit into the rag in his mouth, groaning with the pain underneath him. As the element seared his jacket he smelt burning leather. It was too much. The place would catch fire and he'd die there anyway. He twisted his body. Hitting the floor, he felt the tape loosen on his wrists. He threshed, one shoulder after another working, as he tried to scissor his arms. Suddenly his right hand was free. Nails scrabbled the charred tape from his hands. He tore the strips from eyes, mouth and ankles. His first

149

move was to crawl to the switch. He pounded smouldering cloth and leather into the carpet and lay flat on his
back staring at the underside of the table.

The room was still dark. The curtains drawn. The face
of his watch was cracked but it ticked. Ten minutes to
eleven. With an effort he got up and pulled back the
shades. The skin on his wrists and forearms was angry—
here and there a white pattern showed where the elements
had touched flesh. In the bathroom he found some cotton,
dressed the burns, using the remainder of the adhesive
tape.

Kline had left Drummond's sprawled body as it fell.
The dead face was a caricature of the living man. Fraser
couldn't touch him any more. He stripped a blanket from
Kline's bed and spread it over the body. His jacket was
burnt through at the back. He found one of Kline's
sweaters in a closet—put it on and groped in empty
trouser pockets. The chit for his car was gone—his money
—even Barby's picture. In the kitchen he looked down
at the row of garages. The Jaguar was gone. He sat
down, holding his head in his hands. One side of his face
still sprouted whisker. He moved into the living-room like
a sleepwalker. By now Kline was three hundred miles
over the Atlantic. The odds were with the lawyer. He'd
left one dead man in the flat—another as good as dead. A
locked apartment and no excuse for visitors. Not till the
smell of decomposition aroused the neighbours would the
door be broken in.

He went back to the kitchen. There was a little milk—
some bread. He washed the dry slice down, tasting
nothing. His brain had started to work again. In the
living-room, he lifted the phone from its rest. It buzzed.
He replaced it quickly. No police—not yet. He said the

words aloud very softly. No call from here. Later maybe
—in time for the Yard to have Kline grabbed as he
stepped from the plane. He played out scene after scene
in his head—like an old-fashioned movie with silent jerky
sequences. Kline, flanked by police, pointing. The inn at
Two Bridges. The bar on Jermyn Street. The churchyard where he'd crouched with Drummond. Last of all,
Kline with the gun in his hand.

He felt bandaged wrists nervously. He still had a
chance if he could get out of this place unseen. There
wasn't a single witness to put him anywhere near the
Garrett house. After a while Drummond's body would de-
compose—tenants complain. The smell would be traced
to Kline's flat. Medical evidence could easily establish
the time of Drummond's killing. The porters would be
able to identify first Drummond then himself. Identify
whom! His was one unknown face in seven million.

And Kline . . . Reason fought impulse. Nothing he
might do would give Drummond back his life. Above all,
he had to get out of the building. Kline could wait.

He stepped into the hall and slid a folded piece of paper
down the crack in the door. Its progress stopped at the
level of both Bramah locks. He'd heard right. There was
only one way through that door—with a crowbar. Now
that he had some sort of plan, muscles obeyed brain
promptly. He went into the bathroom. Burnt flesh
protested as he prised the window ajar. Three feet away,
a second window was open at the end of the corridor. A
drain-pipe inches to his right offered purchase. He put
one foot on the lavatory seat—the other on the sill.
Turning in the window space he caught the drain-pipe
with one hand—the open bathroom window with the
other. As he made the long step across, he noticed the

151

face peering up at him. Two floors below, one of the porters was polishing windows. Fraser hauled his other leg over and dropped into the corridor. Kline's front door was on his right. A card was tacked above the mail box.

ALL INQUIRIES SHOULD BE MADE
AT THE DESK DOWNSTAIRS

He ran the thirty feet to the pass door, heart banging. For a second he thought of going up to the roof—hiding there till dark. Instead, he pounded down the stone staircase. Arms outstretched, he hit the pass door at street level. Both porters were waiting for him in the corridor. As he came forward they retreated. A chain and padlock secured the pushbar on the service exit. The short man had the padlock key on a string. The other still wore his overalls. The leather polishing-rag tucked into the waistband. Both men continued to back slowly up the corridor.

Fraser found his voice. " Get out of the way."

" Mr. Kline's bin gone this two hours and more," the short man said warily. " Nobody's got authority to be in his flat." He yelped as Fraser's shoe cut into his shinbone. The window cleaner turned and sprinted for the lobby. " Police! " he bawled. " Stop thief! "

Fraser was a yard beyond when the porter darted behind the reception desk. The man had a police whistle in his mouth. As Fraser went through the revolving doors, the whistle shrilled. He ran out to the forecourt, circling a milk-trolly there. The driver lowered his cage of bottles to the ground. He was young and ready.

" Thief! " gasped Fraser. " Stop thief! " Pointing across the street, he ducked between a truck and cab. Fixing his eyes on the green of Cadogan Square, he pumped his legs till tired muscles could no longer stand it. As he slowed, he looked over his shoulder. A group of people milled in front of the apartment building. The summons of the police whistle was insistent.

Instinct told him to get off the streets and stay there. He'd contact Barby somehow—after dark he could meet her. He was walking out of the square into an Edwardian terrace. The houses red-brick and tall. For thirty years, these had been two and three-flat dwellings. Dark and inconvenient, they still afforded a good address.

He moved as quickly as he could without attracting attention. Any cop looking for him had an easy job on description. The baggy black sweater—bandaged wrists and half-shaved face. There was a possibility that Kline's door had not been broken down yet. Everything depended on what the police made of his connection with Kline. The odds were that they'd try to get hold of the lawyer first.

He was a hundred yards from the crossing when the prowl car turned into the terrace. Without hesitation, he ran up the flight of steps on his right. The hallway was dark. In front of him carpeted stairs led to the upper floors. The heavy street door was caught back on a hook. He slipped behind it, dropped on his heels looking through the crack at the street. The police car drove by slowly. A couple of uniformed men sat in front. In the back, the porter with the medals, between two detectives. The crew of the car was scanning both sidewalks.

His watch had stopped. He guessed five minutes before heaving himself erect. A card, printed in faded ink was pinned to the back of the door.

THIS DOOR TO BE KEPT CLOSED AFTER I I P.M.

153

He slipped out to the hall. Three windowed mail boxes hung on the wall. The door on his right had to lead to the bottom flat. Ahead was a second door with old-fashioned stained-glass panels. He turned the key. Steps led down to an unkept patch of grass with a wooden shed at its end. He went back to the foot of the staircase—stood with a hand on the banister, listening. He went up cautiously, testing each tread. Behind another door on the second story, a child was calling. He climbed on up. The last door was set across the stairs barring his way. A bottle of milk stood at its foot. He tip-toed down, carrying the milk. In the hall he drained the bottle and hid it underneath the garden steps.

The shed was a possible hiding-place till darkness came. But no place to be trapped. He went into the phone-booth. It was dark and smelled of stale tobacco smoke. He dialled O. When the girl answered, he made his voice testy.

" I've had a wrong number twice. Each time I pressed button A. Now I'm out of pennies."

" What number are you calling from ? " the girl asked. He read from the printed notice in front of him. " And what is the number you're calling ? "

He gave Patterson's private office number. " Hold the line," she said, " and I'll try to connect you."

Patterson answered immediately. His voice was anxious. " Where on earth have you been, Kit ? Didn't you get my message ? It's almost one o'clock."

He set the hands of his watch mechanically—gave the winder a few turns. " I couldn't get away, sir. I had . . ."

Patterson interrupted him. " This Garrett woman is creating an uproar. She's phoned three times since ten o'clock—screaming like a lunatic. I've had to give

154

instructions not to put her through any more. She's com-
plaining about the security measures."

Someone had come down the stairs—had passed behind
him to the top of the steps leading to the street. He tucked
his chin into his neck and used the phone to hide his
stubbled cheek.

" They aren't our security measures," he said carefully.
" The underwriters' man simply okayed her installa-
tions."

" Exactly," Patterson's voice was suddenly faint—as if
his hand were cupped over the mouthpiece. He ordered
someone to leave the room. " It's your account, Kit," he
went on. "I want you to have a word with the underwriters.
As you can imagine, they're not at all happy. The thieves
got away with everything we insured."

" What about the police ? "

Patterson grunted. " It's the usual story. A professional job. They expect an early development. How
soon can you get over here, Kit ? Where are you
now ? "

The person had come from the steps back into the hall.
Yet he could see no one in the mirror in front of him. He
took the plunge. " I can't come, sir. I'll have to explain
later. I'm still with the doctor," he finished weakly. For
a moment, he thought that Patterson had hung up. He
heard his father-in-law's breath go in a sigh.

" You may as well know, Kit. I telephoned Doctor
Landers' Clinic an hour ago. He told me he'd never
heard of you."

Fraser wanted to face whoever was behind him yet
dared not turn.

" I haven't said anything to Barby," Patterson said.
" What on earth's possessed you, Kit ? " His voice was

155

gentle. " If you'd tell me, I could help. As it is, you're worrying us all out of our minds."

" You'll know, sir," Fraser started slowly. But there was nothing to say any more. He replaced the receiver and turned.

A small girl in buttoned gaiters was looking up at him. Her straight black hair was worn with a fringe. She whispered in the ear of the battered bear she was holding then spoke politely to Fraser. " Hallo! "

He looked over the top of her head to the door of the bottom flat. It was shut. " Hallo! " he said cautiously.

She came a step closer to him. Her eyes bright and curious. " I live here," she volunteered. " Where do you live ? "

Any moment somebody would come down the stairs— one look at him and there'd be trouble. He spoke very quietly. " A long way away. I'm just visiting."

She nodded. " My Mummy ? " She touched the bandage on his wrist. " What's that ? "

He pulled away. " Just a sore place. No, not your Mummy."

" Mr. Keeble ? " Her small face was triumphant when he made no reply. " Mr. Keeble's in Scotland. With his auntie." Her interest gone, she walked up the stairs. A door opened then shut.

KEEBLE was written above one of the mailboxes. A pile of letters jammed it. He read the address. Peter Keeble, Flat A. A brass ' A ' was nailed on the door to the bottom flat.

There were people moving about on the landing above. He opened the door to the garden and stood behind it. A woman came into view, shadowy through the purple glass. She had the child by the hand and was dressed for

156

the street. He heard the clatter of feet as the girl ran down the steps.

He crept back to the hall. There were two locks on Keeble's door. A Yale and a mortise. The brass surround of the mortise was tarnished—unscratched. The keyhole itself held fluff. He tore a strip from the phone directory, slid it down the door crack. The mortise was unused. He leaned his weight against the door. There was play between tongue and box of the Yale. With a piece of celluloid, he could get in there. Once in, he'd surely be safe till nightfall. Every man on the beat would have his description by now.

He went back to the phone booth and reversed charges to Two Bridges. As soon as he heard Barby answer, he started to speak slowly and distinctly. " Don't ask questions, Barby. Just do what I tell you. Take the first train up to town. Bring the car insurance—the log book and the receipt. The car's in the Aldford Garage—Park Lane. You collect it—tell them the ticket's lost. As soon as it gets dark, drive over to Cadogan Terrace. Park opposite 430. Not outside, opposite! "

She'd let him talk without interruption. Now she had to answer, the words came with difficulty. " What's happened, Kit ? "

" Bring a change of clothing for me—my passport. Some bandages," he said.

" What's happened ? " she repeated. She started to cry softly.

" *Please*, Barby! " he pleaded. " I'm in real trouble. I can't tell you till I see you. Will you do it, Barby ? "

" I'm going to telephone Daddy immediately," she said.

His voice was hopeless. " If you do that, I'm finished,

Barby. I'm in trouble with the police. I've only got one chance—that's if you do exactly as I tell you."

She was suddenly calm. " I'm all right now, Kit. I'll do whatever you say."

" If the phone rings before you leave the house, don't answer," he instructed. He repeated the street and house number.

" I'll be there. I love you," she said quietly. Then the line was dead.

If he was going to break into that empty flat, now was the time. Every minute was a hazard until he was hidden. He looked Keeble's door over again. The play at the lock was definite. Enough force applied would drive the tongue of the Yale against its cup—tear out the screws that held the cup to the door jamb. That would mean noise, though. And the door could be seen from the street. To break it down might take more than one shoulder charge. Mabye two or three.

He went down the steps to the sorry garden. The windows to the Keeble flat were shut tight. He pushed open the shed door. A small grass cutter lay on its side next to a child's tricycle. Yellowed newspapers and broken toys were piled under the cobwebbed window. He searched the shed for a piece of celluloid. There was none. Under the bench at the far end of the shed he found an old hunting mac. The sleeves were too short and the garment stiff and cracked with age. He hid the black sweater under the newspapers and donned the mac. This place was no good to hide. Hours of daylight remained for the child to play in the garden.

He went back to the house. Somehow he had to get hold of celluloid. Sloane Square was no more than three hundred yards away. He tore some of the plaster and cotton from his wrists—used it to cover the bearded side of his face. The upturned mac collar helped cover his jaw-line. He took a careful look at the street. A woman was pushing a baby towards the house. Coming the other way a man followed his broom along the gutter.

Fraser walked quickly. He was covering more ground than necessary but keeping to the crisscross of short streets between Lincoln Street and Sloane Square. He hit the King's Road in front of the barracks. One of the three telephone booths was empty. He ducked in and stood watching. Thirty yards to go. Beyond the railings, a squad of soldiers marched and wheeled. A few passers-by stopped to watch, basking in the autumn sun. After-noon shoppers crowded the opposite sidewalk. He stepped out and walked briskly towards Sloane Square, hugging the wall. At the cafeteria, he turned in. It was hot inside. A railed walk curved in front of the steaming food counter. The customers moved slowly past, pushing their trays to the cashier's desk. There was little room at the tables. Ignoring the line, he took a chair near the barrier. An old man sat across from him, drinking tea noisily. A package of home-wrapped sandwiches was on the marble in front of him.

Fraser spoke impulsively. " Have you got a cigarette to spare ? "

The old man put his cup down and wiped the fog from his steel-rimmed spectacles. The eyes were rheumy but kind. " A fag, mate ? " He groped for a creased package of tobacco and cigarette papers. He watched as Fraser tried to roll one with unskilled fingers. " 'ere, I'll do it," the old man offered. He packed a fat cylinder with dark shag and struck a match for Fraser.

As the younger man took the cigarette, the sleeves of the

mac slid back. Patches of raw skin showed where he had ripped off the plaster.

" Burn ? " said the old man curiously.

Fraser touched his face self-consciously. " I'm going to the doctor."

The old man watched Fraser, bleary-eyed. " That's right, boy. Wants seeing to, a thing like that. At the 'orspittle," he added. He waited a second then guessed. " You off a ship, boy ? "

Fraser nodded. The menu card was in a frame at his elbow. A thickness of celluloid protected it from greasy fingers.

The old man sucked the last of his tea and creaked up. " Good luck, mate," he said and shuffled away. The sandwiches and packet of shag were where he had left them. Holding the menu under the table, Fraser pulled the sheet of celluloid from the frame. He pocketed the food and tobacco and started for the door. The sandwiches were a godsend. He'd eaten little since the day before.

The fresh air was good after the humidity of the cafe. He loosened the collar of the mac. A dozen yards away, a newsvender was fitting a poster into a wire cage.

West End Jewel Robbery

Fraser walked by the stacked newspapers, reading the headline as he passed. A group of pedestrians was waiting to use the crossing. He sidled into the centre of the group. He was half-way to the other side of the street when he saw the two men standing there.

Both were tall and carried raincoats. They had half-turned and were staring in his direction. He pushed out of the crowd and ran round a bus to the sidewalk. As he scrambled through the bus queue, he saw the two men sprinting after him.

The swing door of the department store was ten feet away. He hit its middle with his shoulder, scattering the people in the lobby. Another fifteen yards and he was in the furnishing hall, surrounded by rugs and carpets. On his right, a group of people waited by the elevators. He ran for the stairs, side-stepping the advancing sales clerk. The hall of the store was open to the road—each floor a gallery served by both staircase and elevators. As he turned the first corner he saw the men from the street below. They were sprinting up the stairs, thirty feet behind, wasting no breath in shouting.

He took the next flight, two steps at a time, toppling the showstands as he went. Suitcases, rugs and trunks clattered down the stairs after him. Swerving left through racks of dresses, he broke for the rear of the building and a fire exit. Shouts and a woman's scream followed him. An office door opened immediately in front of him. A man came out, his face indignant. Seeing Fraser, he made a half-hearted attempt to block the fire-exit. Fraser straightened him with a Rugby hand-off and ducked into the empty office. As he locked the door, he saw the man picking himself up.

The room was small. A desk and chair under the window. A few files against a wall. He dragged the desk and chair across the floor—jammed them end to end from door to window. The door handle turned then the whole frame shivered under the impact of somebody's weight. A man's voice cut through the shouting confusion with authority. " Is there any other way he can get out ? "

Net curtains hung across the window from ceiling to radiator. He tried the window catch. It did not move.

161

He gripped it with both hands. Straining till the vein on his forehead stood out. As the catch gave, the windows swung in, catching against the wall. He craned down at the street. The noise beyond the office door had stopped. There was a sudden clamour that retreated as the people there ran for the staircase.

Twenty feet below, pedestrians were passing by, window-shopping. None raised a head. He wrenched the curtains down and knotted them to the radiator. Climbing out to the sill, he lowered himself hand over hand till he hung suspended, legs dangling four yards above the sidewalk. He dropped, sprawling on the cement at a woman's feet. Her hand went to her mouth and she watched him struggling to pull himself up. Somebody helped him from behind. There was a murmur of concern and alarm. He shook himself free and ran across the street. Every yard was an effort. He trotted slowly up the cobbled mews. He had no will to look behind. Fancy peopled the mews with running figures, arms outstretched to grab him

He turned blindly into a row of tall houses. A few yards away a boy carrying a basket mounted the steps. His bicycle was propped against the kerb. As Fraser climbed to the saddle, the boy turned his head. His shout followed the bicycle round the corner.

Fraser pumped desperately—head down, standing on the pedals. He drove his legs with new-found energy. Racing round the square he swerved erratically as he braked for the turn. Cadogan Terrace was empty. He rode the last fifty yards cautiously—ready to wheel in any direction. Wobbling to a stop, he took one last look at the street. Then he hauled the bicycle to the shelter of the hall. When he'd propped it out of sight from the sidewalk, he ran upstairs. There was no sound from either flat. In the garden shed, he stripped off the mac. His body was sour with sweat and fright. The adhesive tape on his face was peeling. Wincing, he tore it free of the stubble.

Using the rusty garden shears, he trimmed the piece of celluloid. Shaping it to a rough oblong, two inches by six. The corners rounded at one end. It was a quarter past three. The bicycle in the hall would mean little to the woman with the child—but the sooner he was in that flat, the better. He stood at the shed window, watching the backs of the neighbouring houses. It all looked safe enough. He ran up the steps to the hall.

Left hand flat against the top of Keeble's door, he held the celluloid in his right. He forced the strip down the crack to the box of the lock, pulled it back fractionally then in. He felt the rounded end engage against the spring-loaded tongue. Working the strip forward, he leaned his weight against the top half of the door. The tongue of the lock retracted slowly under pressure from the pliable celluloid. And suddenly, without sound or fuss, the door was open.

The flat was dark and needed air. Three doors on his right were closed. A coat and umbrella hung on a stand in front of him. He wheeled the bicycle into the flat. Kneeling at the closed door, he squinted through the unused keyhole. Nothing moved in the hall outside. A car horn sounded and somebody passed on the street. Then silence.

He opened the first closed door. Big bay windows overlooked the terrace. Without disturbing the drawn inner curtains, he had an uninterrupted view left and right for a hundred yards. This was a big room—well furnished as a man living alone might want it. Bright chair covers matched that on the low divan. A desk with telephone stood on one side of the windows—on the other, a clothes closet and tallboy. A buff carpet spread from wall to wall. Lighted and with the enormous heater going, it would be a cheerful room. He went out to the passage.

The other two doors opened on a kitchen and bathroom. Originally, this had been one room, overlooking the garden. Now a partition divided it. The glass in both windows was opaque. He searched the wall cabinet in the bathroom. There was everything there that he needed. A couple of old safety razors—blades to fit them. Behind a pile of bottles was a small first-aid kit with burn dressings. A gas water-heater hung suspended over one end of the tub.

A turn of the hot water faucet and in five minutes the tub would hold steaming relief. He took his hand from the tap. The people next door were no more than a double course of bricks away. Sound of a bath filling would carry. The neighbours might well know of Keeble's absence. He had to keep the flat free of flushing cisterns—banging doors. Any sound that could not be accounted for innocently.

He heated water on the kitchen stove and scraped his face clean. Then he dressed his wrists, dabbing iodine on the places where the skin was broken. Back in the bedroom, he went through Keeble's correspondence. Most of it was from a firm of Calcutta jute brokers. He ploughed through it till he found the Edinburgh postmark. The letter was written in spiky backhand. He took it over to the light. The writer had little to say beyond offering to put Keeble up for two weeks before he left for the Orient.

Fraser pulled out the desk drawers. Bank returns—bills—stationery. In the bottom drawer he found a passport tucked in a leather case. He opened it. The face on

the picture was solemn—caught in the stiff pose favoured
by passport photographers. The man wore spectacles.

He carried it to the end of the divan and sat down,
turning the pages of the stiff blue folder.

Profession ....*Jute importer*
Place & Date of Birth ......*Edinburgh,* 18 *January,* 1918
Height ....5'11"
Colour of Eyes ....*Blue*
Colour of Hair ....*Brown*
Special Peculiarities ....*None*

Keeble's signature was neat underneath.

He riffled the pages. The document was valid for three
years more. A block of Far East visas covered four of the
pink sheets. He took a pair of sun-glasses from the litter
on top of the desk. Putting them on, he stood in front of
the mirror. The shape of his face wasn't unlike that on
the passport photograph. With a hat and the right sort of
spectacles he could get by. Age and description fitted him
as well as Keeble. He sat down again. There was another
document in the leather holder—Keeble's birth certificate. Fraser replaced the passport. These papers could
take him round the world if he handled them right.

The clatter of feet outside took him to the window. The
small girl was skipping up the steps. Her mother followed,
laughing. Tiptoeing to the end of the passage, he waited
till he heard the door upstairs open and shut. Back in the
bedroom, he rolled a cigarette and lay on the divan.

Now that the initial shock of Drummond's death was
over, the implications were clearer. He was more than a
thief—he'd witnessed a murder. The two things were in-
separable. Escape was the only answer to both predica-

165

ments. Somehow, he had to get out of England quickly. But before that—long before—he had to telephone Scotland Yard.

He rolled over, staring at the phone on the desk. Not here—nor the booth outside. His message would send fifty police cars to its source. He had to wait till it was dark. He sat on the edge of the divan. This flat had to be left wrecked. He'd take the sort of things a chance prowler might steal. Clothes, the cheque-book in the drawer—the camera. Anything of value that might be easily carried. One of the front windows could be left open. The police had to be stopped from identifying the housebreaker with the man from Kline's apartment.

He stubbed the soggy cigarette butt—carefully leaving it where it might be seen. He remembered the child upstairs—her interest in his wrists. Hell, a child's memory was short. By the time the police got around to her—if they ever did—their questioning would only confuse her. With luck, he'd be out of the country by then. That's what he needed—luck and Barby's help. Keeble's passport would take him out of England. Between Hamburg and Ostend, a dozen ports of call for freighters offered safety. Waterfront bars, where the only passport needed was the price asked.

He started prowling about the flat impatiently. The kitchen cupboards offered the sparse provender of a bachelor flat. A few cans of food—some tea and sugar—no milk. He sat down on the bed again and ate the old man's sandwiches.

The sun had vanished behind the roofs opposite. Already the sky was darkening. To kill time, he set the scene for the police. Pulling out drawers, rifling cupboards. Some of Keeble's belongings he packed in a case.

When he had done, the room was a jumble of papers and clothing.

It was gone four. By now, Kline's plane was a thousand miles away—high in the sun, heading south. An escape that must have been planned weeks ago. With one dead man behind him—another due to die, Kline would use every angle to break trail once he reached his destination. But till he reached it, he'd feel safe.

Fraser carried the bag to the passage—set it by the bicycle. Suddenly the phone in the bedroom started to ring. He stayed where he was until it stopped. He sat by the window, watching the street from behind the curtain. Five minutes went by and the phone rang again. This time, in the flat above. He heard the woman cross the room to answer it.

Outside, it was getting darker by the minute. Every sound—every movement—a source of possible danger. Suddenly the sidewalks were brighter. The street lamps had been turned on. A girl hurried along. As she came up the steps, he ran into the passage. One of the mailboxes was being unlocked. Crouched at the keyhole, he watched the girl climb the staircase. The top flat, he guessed. Probably there was still a husband to come for the woman with the child. Then the house would be full.

The standard across the street threw a shaft of light a foot wide through the bedroom windows. He hitched one of the heavy lined curtains a fraction. On a chair behind it, he waited for Barby.

It was almost six. A man carrying a brief-case hurried into the house. Another ten minutes and a girl followed. Top flat, he thought. One after another, the neighbouring churches struck the hour. He switched on the radio by Keeble's bed, throttling the volume. Ear close to the speaker, he listened to the emergency calls. The police messages. They were meaningless. The announcer's tone was brisk—" And now for the news! " Fraser silenced the set.

Where in hell was Barby . . . . Trains ran every half-hour from Two Bridges to Waterloo. He padded about the room nervously. The television was loud upstairs—the child thudded from one wall to the other. With luck, they were all in for the night. If not, he had to risk running into somebody in the hall outside, later. On an impulse he sat down at the desk, addressed an envelope to Keeble, disguising the handwriting. A blank sheet of notepaper completed the letter. He put it in his pocket.

At the window again, he dragged the minutes out. Suddenly the familiar shape of the Buick brought him to his feet. He stood motionless, hidden in the folds of the curtains. The Buick's stoplights glowed red. A front window was lowered. Hatless, Barby leaned out scanning the house numbers. Obeying his instructions, she was parked on the opposite side of the street, facing north. As he watched, the window went up. For a second, her face was visible in the flame from her lighter. Then no more than the glow from her cigarette.

He waited a full five minutes, watching both car and street. It all looked innocent enough. The few pedestrians scuttled by, indifferent as they passed the parked car.

He ran to the flat door—opened it—leaving the catch up on the Yale lock. Cautiously, he wheeled the bicycle into the outer hall. As he carried it down the steps to the street, Barby touched the horn. He looked up at the curtained windows of the nearby houses, his hand a frantic appeal for silence. He pushed the machine across the road.

" Give me the car keys."

Unlocking the big trunk, he pushed the bicycle in. The front wheels and handlebars cocked at an angle. Metal crunched as he forced down the top of the trunk. With a last look at the windows of 430 he climbed in beside Barby.

" Make two left turns, then into Cadogan Square," he ordered. The car jerked forward, transmission juddering as she fumbled the clutch. His hand gripped her knee. " Easy, darling, easy! "

Two hundred yards north, she manœuvred the nose of the Buick towards the railings. She killed the motor and sat with hands folded in her lap. Her whole body was trembling. He caught her close to him, holding her till the shake subsided. There was enough light from the street lamp to see her face. Her eyes were dry—her lips out of control. Beyond words, he kissed her roughly. They sat in silence till he touched her cheek. She took his wrist in her hands.

He shook his head. " That's nothing. Barby—things are bad . . ." This was hopeless. He had no idea how to tell her. " They couldn't be worse."

Her grip tightened. " For God's sake *tell* me, Kit! " she pleaded.

Very gently, he unfastened her fingers. " It'll have to wait till later, Barby. Has anyone been to the house since I left—or phoned ? "

" No. Only Daddy. He phoned three times to-day. The last to tell me he'd spoken to you. Kit . . ." She lowered her head. He put his hand under her chin, raising it. She dabbed at her eyes with a tissue. " I'll be all right now," she insisted. Her voice was resolute.

" Wasn't there a package for me ? "

She nodded. "It's there." She pointed to the back seat. "I brought it with me."

"What kept you so long?"

She took the key from the ignition. "The garage. They didn't want to release the car. I had to show all the papers. Even see the manager and sign a form."

"Did you bring the clothes?" he asked suddenly.

She nodded, her face fighting the tears. A soft-topped bag lay on the back seat. He leaned over and opened it. Suit, shoes, shirt. An overcoat. Wrapped in brown paper, the wire recorder and reel. He pulled on the overcoat.

"I've got to make a phone call," he said quietly. "Once I've done it, the police are going to be looking for a murderer."

Her breath caught. "Oh no—Kit!"

"I've seen a man killed," he said flatly. "Now listen—I've got to make the call out of this district. Drive towards Kensington. We'll find the right place to phone. As soon as it's done, drive back here as fast as you can."

They were almost at Pont Street. "Turn left," he said quietly. As the car passed the apartment building he looked up at the end of the wing. Someone had shut Kline's bathroom window.

"Exhibition Road." His voice was a croak.

They drove in silence till the vast stretch was in front of them. Left and right loomed the museums, dark and deserted. A hundred yards on, he touched her arm. Two phone booths stood back to back at the entrance to a mews.

She was watching him nervously. He nodded across the street.

"This'll do. I'm going to be two minutes. Keep the

motor running. As soon as I'm back in the car, head for Cadogan Square. . . ."

She was huddled over the wheel—hair hiding her eyes. " Be careful," she whispered.

He walked over to the booth, his footsteps echoing down the mews. Pulling on gloves, he opened the door. The lights of the car seemed far away. For a second he hesitated, finger over the dial—then spun it—WHI—1212. The answer came almost immediately. A calm authoritative voice. " New Scotland Yard."

The words he'd rehearsed were gone. He tried desperately to remember them.

" New Scotland Yard," repeated the voice patiently.

He cleared his throat. " Four hundred, Pont Street—Tower Lodge. There's a dead man in flat thirty-nine. The man you want's on a plane for El Salvador." He spelt Kline's name. " Flight 703—Central American Airlines."

The voice at the other end was unhurried. " Where are you speaking from, sir ? " The metallic summons persisted. " Will you repeat that address again, please ? "

He put the receiver back on the rest and hurried up the mews. The car moved off as he took his seat. Once in the plaited traffic at South Kensington, he felt safer. No one had seen him leave the booth.

In the quiet of the square, he took both her hands. " Listen, darling. We're going back to the house where you parked. When we get there, we go straight up the steps and through the first door to the right." Her eyes never left his face. " If we meet anyone on the way in, I'll drop this in the mailbox." He showed her the dummy envelope. " We'll have to come straight out—circle the block and try again. We've got to get inside that flat. Have you got it ? "

171

Sense of what he was saying seemed to escape her. When he repeated the question, she buttoned her coat and took her handbag. " I'm ready."

A rising east wind sent the dead leaves scurrying across the square. He tucked his chin in the upturned coat collar. " Let's go! "

Carrying the suitcase in his left hand, he held her arm tight with the other. They walked away from the car quickly, heads down. At the steps to the house, he pulled his arm free and found the dummy envelope. The hall light had been lit but Keeble's door was as it had been left. He shut it behind them, fastening the flimsy bolt. She was moving about uncertainly in the dark—the coat stand tottered.

He made a sound of warning. " I can't see! " she whispered. " Put on the light! "

He found her hand and led her into the bedroom. He pulled her down beside him on the divan. " This flat's empty," he said quietly. " But I had to break into it to get away from the police."

She looked round the dim room, shaking her hair back mechanically. With a quick movement, he buried his face against her breast, blotting out everything except the feel of her. Warm fingers were stroking the hair on his neck. Her voice was soft with understanding. " Whatever it is you've done, Kit, I'll help you. But I've got to know what it is." She pulled his head up so that she could see his eyes. In the light from the street, her face was tender. " I'll help you, darling," she repeated.

They sat close together, lost to the sound of the music upstairs—the danger outside. He told his tale without emotion. From the meeting with Kline in the inn. He

172

offered no excuse nor did she move to question till he was done.

She picked at the bedcover. Suddenly she looked up, her hand touching her forehead. " I can't seem to think for the moment. It's all too horrible. Worst of all—I feel I'm responsible."

He shook his head. " One way or another, we're all responsible, Barby. The only way out is to run. As fast as we can, but *run!* "

" I don't believe that," she said fiercely. " People— even the police—aren't as stupid or heartless as you think. You've been *blackmailed*, Kit. Don't you see." She jerked his arm impatiently.

Bitterness seeped into his voice. " There isn't going to be any charity in this deal, Barby. There's a dead man in Kline's flat. For the police that's the only thing that matters."

She let his arm go—her voice desperately reasonable. " But you didn't kill him, Kit! "

All these years he must have had a doubt in the strength of Barby's love. Like someone with a perverse will to lose. He knew now that she would never fail him. And the understanding was too late.

" I didn't kill him," he repeated. " But people will say I had every reason to! " He turned to face her. " I'm in too deep, Barby. All that's going to count are the facts. The facts as the police will see them."

" No! " she whispered, shaking her head.

" Yes! " he insisted gently. " You know the one thing nobody will forget. I could have said 'no' to Kline back in the inn in Two Bridges. But I didn't."

A door upstairs opened. He tiptoed to the window and watched the man cross the street to mail his letters. He

173

stood motionless behind the curtain till the whistle on the stairs grew faint. Then the door was closed again.

She said his name softly. He sat down beside her. "We've got to go to Daddy at once. He'll know what to do and he'll help. I *know* he'll help, Kit."

He found her bag, cigarettes—lit two. "Help!" he repeated. "You're out of your mind! What can he do, Barby! He'll go to the police as soon as he knows the truth. Sure. Nothing'll stop him doing that. Do you realise what this means for him—not just for me but *him*!" He was shaking. "Barby . . ." he started compassionately.

She hunched on the bed, small and miserable. "It's no use, Kit. I . . . I can't even think. . . ."

He put an arm round her. "I've got a plan that gives us all a chance. But you've got to be with me, Barby. Not against me."

She moved her head impatiently. "How can you *say* that!" She dragged deep on her cigarette. Her eyes were unwavering in its glow. "I'm your wife, Kit. That means more to me than you'll ever know."

He pulled her down beside him, his mouth against her hair. "We've got to get out of England. Both of us. Before Kline has a chance to talk. He's going to try to bluff his way out of all this. He won't open up till he realises they're going to bring him back here. That's going to take time," he urged. "Enough time for us to be somewhere they'll never find us."

She moved restlessly. "What about Daddy—this man's going to tell the police everything—lie to protect himself. And you'll have run away. You're going to leave Daddy to face all that on his own?"

He stared at the ceiling. "Supposing I was dead?"

he said quietly. He felt her body stiffen. " Supposing everybody *thought* I was dead! Whatever Kline says, it'll leave your father a victim of circumstance. The police will know that I fooled him all these years. Maybe it *will* mean retirement. But he's respected, Barby. They'll make it easy for him. People like that stick together," he urged.

She broke his hold to lie silent, head averted. " How could people *think* you were dead ? " she asked finally.

" It's easy. We'll drive down to the coast in the morning. I'll rent some sort of sailing-boat. I'll go out in it and never come back. And make sure they know who I am." He tried to impart some of his own confidence. " I'll take a lifebelt with me. Check the right places for currents. God, Barby, there are spots where chances of a body being found are one in twenty. Either it drifts out to sea or the tide and the rocks finish it."

" And what do we do for the rest of our lives—run ? " Her voice rose. " Always hiding—never knowing when you'll be arrested! " She was suddenly calm. " That's not escape, Kit. It's worse—far worse—than anything that can happen to you here." She propped herself on an elbow. " I'll never leave you," she said solemnly. " I just want you to do the right thing."

" The right thing! " What did she *know* of right and wrong! " I'm going, Barby," he said deliberately. " You'll have to make up your mind whether you come with me or not."

She lay absolutely still. Then she started to laugh. A laugh that shook itself into stifled moans. He'd never seen her hysterical before. Any moment and neighbours would be pounding on the door. He put his hand over her mouth, forcing her back on the pillows till she gasped for breath. She was quiet again after a while.

175

Salt stung his eyes. He could not see her properly.

" Well, Barby ? " he said gently.

Her head moved on the pillow. " I love you, Kit."
She said no more.

They stripped to their underclothes and huddled, silent
in the bed. He dozed off with his arm dead under her
weight. Twice during the night he woke to startled re-
collection. His head was close to her breast. She was
watching him. " Go to sleep," she whispered, with the
sound of her voice he was able to forget and closed his eyes
with confidence.

Far over the roofs, the dark sky was streaked with
violet. The street lamps still burned. Barby was sleeping
heavily, her eyes smudged where the make-up had run.
He touched her shoulder. Her fingers uncurled and she
stretched easily. She sat up, taking in the tumbled bed,
the chaos of the room. He slid an arm round her. " It's
still early—nearly seven. Try to get a little rest for another
half-hour."

He fumbled his way round the tiny kitchen, boiling
water. He shaved by the flare of the gas burners. The
feel of fresh linen—his own clothes—was reassuring.
Water was running in the upstairs bathroom. The child's
voice was shrill. Somebody opened a window. He went
back to the bedroom. Barby had dressed. She was kneeling by the desk, sorting order from the strewn papers.

" Leave it," he said. " Just get yourself ready to go."

He opened the window nearest to the street door. A
long stride would do it. From the steps to the window sill.
It would be no trick for a night-time prowler, satisfied the
flat was empty.

The door in the house opposite came ajar enough for
an arm to pose a couple of empty milk bottles on the step.

A cat arched its back, rubbing against the railings. The street was bleak and grey. Barby was standing behind him, her face almost hidden in the big roll collar. He gave her the suitcase she had brought, now empty. " You wait in the car," he said. " I'll be twenty minutes."

He led her out to the hall—listened by the stairs then opened the street door. " Twenty minutes," he whispered. He ran back to the bedroom to watch till she had turned the corner. A red van had stopped, twenty yards away. The driver unlocked the mailbox, scooping its contents into a bag. He dragged the bag across the sidewalk to the waiting van. Eight o'clock.

He found the passport and birth certificate. Then wrapping his hands in two of Keeble's shirts, he went round the flat wiping and polishing every surface that Barby or he had touched. Taking Keeble's suitcase from the passage, he shut the front door after him. As he walked down the steps, he heard a girl calling good-bye from the upper stairs.

The bag was heavy with junk. He kept shifting it from one hand to the other. Twenty yards away at the inter-section, a uniformed policeman stepped to the centre of the road. Arms held at a quarter-past twelve, he blocked non-existent traffic to let a group of school-children scamper across the street. He stepped back to the side-walk, his face incongruously young under the helmet. He met Fraser's nod with a self-conscious grin.

Leaves littered the top of the Buick—the windows were clouded with frost. He opened the trunk and wedged the suitcase on top of the bicycle. Barby had the motor running. He took his place next to her.

" The police aren't looking for *me* yet," he assured her. " They're looking for a man without a name."

177

She waited for the wipers to clear the windshield. The strain was showing in the set of her mouth—the nervous snatch in her fingers as she tried to light her cigarette. But the expression on her face was one he had reason to remember. Months ago, he'd watched, panic-stricken, as a half-schooled hunter threw her five times one Sunday afternoon. Deaf to his entreaty, she'd picked herself up—limped across to the waiting horse. When she'd hauled herself up in the saddle, her voice wavered but not her eyes.

" He's *going* to jump! " she assured him. He stood clear as she'd backed the bay for a run. And suddenly they were both over the hurdle.

He took the cigarette from her mouth and kissed her. " Scared ? " he said softly.

She nodded, holding his arm tight. " I'm worried about Daddy, Kit. He's probably been phoning Two Bridges all night. He'll be frantic if he doesn't hear from either of us."

He thought for a moment. " You're right. You'd better go to see him right away. Tell him anything you like—anything that'll hold him for just one more day."

She stopped the motor and sat with her hands in her lap. Very slowly, she opened her bag. There was a letter in an inside compartment. He recognised his own hand-writing. " This came for you yesterday morning," she said quietly.

The Reading Room in Canada House was a lifetime away. He reached to take the letter—rip it in two.

She stopped him. " It's really to me—isn't it ? " He moved his head. " Then let me keep it," she said. He made no move to stop her as she put the envelope back in its place—unopened and unread.

She worried her lip. " You realise Daddy's going to wonder why *you* haven't gone to see him." He made no answer. " You're his son, Kit," she said gently. " It isn't too late."

" I'm a liar," he answered. " And that's how he'll have to remember me." His bandaged wrists were tight under his shirt cuffs. He eased them, wincing. " Tell him I've been acting strangely ever since I got home. You're going to take me to see a doctor. No! Say, I've got to see some people—you're driving me there. We'll both be round this evening."

She pulled her gloves on. " Whatever you did, he'd forgive, Kit. For your own sake, not mine. But you're not even going to give him the chance."

Rather than meet her look, he bent to straighten a kink in the carpet. He sat up, his face hard. " Have *I* had a chance ? " he asked bitterly.

The fight seemed gone from her. She started backing out the car. " I'll go there right away, before he leaves for the office. Where are you going, Kit ? "

He stretched his legs, wriggling lower in his seat. " There's a lot to do." He checked his watch. " Drop me at Piccadilly Circus. I'll be waiting in the lobby of the Tate Gallery at eleven o'clock."

She backed to the kerb. Slouched as he was, she forced his head round so that she could see his face. " Will you *be* there, Kit ? "

" If I'm not," he said steadily, " it'll mean that the police have got me. Then you'll have to do the best you can—for both of us. But I'll be there, Barby," he repeated. " It's a promise." Memory prompted. " I've got no money." She gave him her wallet.

The lights were against them at Piccadilly Circus. He

179

slipped from the car to join the crowd jamming the subway entrance. Downstairs, he checked in Keeble's suitcase. Crossing the booking-hall, he threw away the ticket. He climbed the steps to Shaftesbury Avenue. Fighting his way through the crowd of office workers, he bought a paper from the corner vendor. He stood in a doorway, shielding his face with the damp newspaper.

The bald account was on the front page. MAN FOUND SHOT IN WEST END FLAT. No names were mentioned—nothing but the address and a description of Drummond. The last sentence was cryptic. " The police have not ruled out the possibility of foul play."

A small man in a bowler hat had stopped in front of the shop doorway. He looked curiously at Fraser. There was a bunch of keys in his hand. Muttering an apology, Fraser hurried away.

Every cop in uniform would have a description of the man who had left Kline's flat. It was fourteen hours since he'd phoned the Yard. Kline could have talked. He turned back into the optician's doorway. The man was still opening his store.

" I want a pair of glasses—plain lens. Something that will keep the wind from my eyes." Fraser kept his accent neutral. " They water."

The salesman was professionally wise. " You probably need something a little stronger than plain lens, sir. If your eyes water it may be a sign of weakness. We'll soon tell." He started towards an inner room.

" Plain lens," said Fraser definitely. He chose thick frames, and put them on. Outside, he stopped a passing cab.

As the cab reached Kensington High Street, he tapped

on the partition. " Let me off somewhere I can get a cup of coffee."

It was nine-fifteen by the Public Library clock when he climbed the steps. The subdued assistant was helpful. After a while she struggled across the empty Reference Room. Her arms held a pile of books—Admiralty Charts. He read steadily for a half-hour, using his imagination.

He knew exactly where he must hire a boat. The charts made it clear. Somewhere just north of the Dover —Cap Gris Nez line. A body three miles out in the main Channel stream would be washed up either on the Dutch, German or Norwegian coastline. Never on any English shore. And the police would know it.

He left the library. A line of parked cabs was in the centre of the street. As he stepped from the kerb, the deep voice boomed behind him. " Police Officer. May I have a word with you! "

He turned, sick with sudden nausea. It was Bannon, the phoney cop, showing large teeth in a grin. " Gave you a start," he said knowingly. " You're a godsend." He propped a foot on the kerb, blocking Fraser's way. " I've been phoning Kline for a day. The swine's either dead or drunk. He owed me a tenner—from the other day. How about letting me have it. You can get it from Kline when you see him."

They'd moved back on the sidewalk, standing in front of the library steps. He watched Bannon appraisingly. The red jovial face showed only satisfaction. The man couldn't have seen a morning paper yet. " Go round to Kline's flat at twelve and you'll find him in. Whether he answers the phone or not, he'll be there." Without waiting for an answer, he walked over to the cab at the head of the line.

181

The bank fronted the sweep of Cockspur Street. A modern freestone building with a glass front. A porter was shouldering back the grille as Fraser's cab stopped. A few anxious-eyed customers pushed their way in before him, cheques in hand.

He chose the cashier he did not know. " Let me have a credit balance, will you ? " The man came back to slide a folded slip across the counter. Fraser carried it to a desk. He read the paper as a man does bad news. £637 15s. 2d.

It was better than he had expected. He wrote a cash cheque for six hundred pounds. " Fives," he told the cashier. " As new as possible."

The money made a wad less than an inch thick. He divided its bulk between hip pockets. " Ask Mr. Byrant if he can see me for a moment," he said.

The wall of the manager's office was hung with plaques bearing the arms of the Provinces. Fraser sat at the desk. Six years since he had first come in here. Carrying a commission cheque. Byrant—the room itself—had changed little since then.

The manager's welcome was warm. " Morning, Mr. Fraser. We see too little of you these days! "

Fraser crossed his ankles. " I want you to sell out whatever stock you're holding for me. I'll sign the papers now."

Byrant opened a folder, scanned the typewritten sheets. " Sell ? " he repeated dubiously. " I'm not sure it wouldn't be better to take advice before we commit our-selves." He dragged over a sheaf of broking reports. " It's not the moment for marketing Industrials."

" I want them sold to-day," repeated Fraser. " And the

yield transferred to my wife's credit. Have you got the address of her bank ? "

Byrant touched a button—gave the girl who answered it an instruction. He went back again to Fraser's file. " Yes, we have a note of it here. Mrs. Barbara Fraser. It's still the Two Bridges address ? "

Fraser leaned over the desk, signing where the manager's finger pointed. Byrant came to the door of the office with him. He was diffident. " I have to say this— you're not thinking of closing your account, are you, Mr. Fraser ? There's nothing the bank can do . . ." he shrugged, " or *should* have done ? "

Fraser hesitated, then gave a hand to Byrant. " I'm taking a trip," he said. " You can't always be certain of coming back."

It was a short step to the travel agency at the bottom of the Haymarket. A girl at the end of the counter was unoccupied.

" I want a ticket on this evening's ferry from Folkestone to Boulogne," he said. " Is there any difficulty getting on ? "

She smiled, shaking her head. " Not at this time of the year. First or second ? "

" Second," he answered. He'd feel safer in a crowd. There was still the problem of Barby's ticket to be solved. He dared not risk travelling with her.

" And your name, sir ? "

" Peter Keeble," he said evenly.

He hurried across the square to the lower end of the Strand. He found what he wanted in one of the Government Surplus stores. A seaman's sweater, thick serge trousers, an ex-navy life jacket. It was twenty to eleven when he hailed the cab to take him to the Embankment.

The driver took him through the park. Wedged in the corner of the back seat, he watched. The wide Mall, its trees black in the wintry sunshine. His regiment had marched there, pipes skirling. Past packed stands, white with the welcome of a thousand handkerchiefs. To a palace bedecked with the flags of the Commonwealth. And the medal. That night had been made sober by his father's cable of congratulations.

"Well done stop Vincit qui se vincit stop Father." *He conquers who conquers himself*. . . .

He sat upright, dismissing every memory that might weaken his purpose. The man was driving fast, wheeling his cab through the back streets to the river front. As they neared the pile of the Tate Gallery, Fraser stopped the cab.

"This'll do!" He gave the man some coins. When the cab was gone, he turned the corner and climbed the steps to the main entrance.

The clock in the lobby showed a couple of minutes before the hour. He stood by the rack of postcards, staring at the river beyond the Embankment. It was gone eleven when a cab pulled into the forecourt and Barby got out.

In spite of himself, his mouth was acid with fear. Indifferent to the attendants behind him, he peered through the glass door, scanning the street. Why had she come in a cab . . . there could only be one reason—she was afraid of being followed! His ears strained for the gong of a police car. East and west, the sidewalks were deserted save for a man feeding the pigeons.

Fraser checked his parcel of clothing. As Barby came through the door, he stepped from the shelter of the post-card stand. She was hatless, her face strained. The freckles on her cheekbones dark against her pallor. He took her arm, guiding her through the turnstile. They found a bench in a room hung with modern paintings. Through the window a barge chugged downstream, headed for wharves hidden in haze. And maybe the open sea beyond, he thought.

He locked both hands on his knees, tightening his grip till the blood left his fingertips. " What's happened ? " he whispered. " Where's the car ? "

She lifted her head slowly. " Kline's dead," she said deliberately.

Her words made no sense. His voice cracked, incredulous. " *Kline!* "

She answered him quietly. " He was arrested leaving the plane in Salvador." Her hands moved in nervous explanation. " He shot himself at the airport. They found Mrs. Garrett's jewellery in his luggage. That's why they phoned Daddy. They told him they'd had a call about Kline last night—an anonymous one."

He slouched, head down, weak with relief. When he was sure of himself, he looked up at her. " Kline's dead, Barby! And without talking! " His voice broke. " You know what this means! " He was suddenly cautious, watching the doors to the other rooms. " Nobody'll ever know," he said softly. " Not even your father." He wanted to hold her. The look on her face stopped him.

She chose her words carefully, keeping her eyes on his. " Daddy does know, Kit. I told him."

Shock brought him to his feet. He stood over her, his mouth thin with anger. She waited without fear or defiance. After a moment he slumped back on the bench. It was over. He was finished. Yet he had to know why she had done this to him.

He shoved a hand through his hair, trying to read the

answer in her eyes. She made no move to touch him. It was as though she must deny herself all vestige of appeal.

She spoke unevenly, fighting the shake in her fingers. " He still loves you and trusts you, Kit. He's an old man and our happiness means more to him, even, than the end of a career."

Colour blurred in the canvas in front of him. He was unable to keep the bitterness from his voice. " What's *your* idea of making us all happy—ruining three people's lives when its no longer necessary ? "

She shook her head. " It doesn't matter what my idea is, Kit. For the first time—ever since this dreadful business started—you're the one who's got to make the decision. Daddy will never tell the police about your part in the robbery." She shrugged. " You said it yourself—nobody's going to know unless you tell them." She took his hands suddenly, holding them close to her. " I love you too, Kit. Whatever you decide to do, I'll stick with you. If you're going to run, then I must run with you." Footsteps sounded on the polished boards. She let go his hands.

They made their way out. At the top of the steps, he stopped. " You really mean that ? That you'll go with me ? "

Wind blew a handful of hair across her eyes. She pushed it back and he saw she was crying. " I mean it," she answered. Head high, she followed him down the steps.

A cab slowed as Fraser flagged it. He opened the door, touching her cheek with his mouth then climbed in after her. He pulled back the glass partition, bending forward so that the driver heard his direction. " New Scotland Yard."

››› If you've enjoyed this book and would like to discover more great vintage crime and thriller titles, as well as the most exciting crime and thriller authors writing today, visit: **›››**

The Murder Room
Where Criminal Minds Meet

themurderroom.com